A
Purrfect
Alibi

BOOKS BY LEIGHANN DOBBS

THE OYSTER COVE GUESTHOUSE (CAT COZY MYSTERY SERIES)
A Twist in the Tail
A Whisker in the Dark
A Purrfect Alibi

MYSTIC NOTCH (CAT COZY MYSTERY SERIES)
Ghostly Paws
A Spirited Tail
A Mew to a Kill
Paws and Effect
Probable Paws
Whisker of a Doubt
Wrong Side of the Claw

BLACKMOORE SISTERS (COZY MYSTERY SERIES)
Dead Wrong
Dead & Buried
Dead Tide
Buried Secrets
Deadly Intentions
A Grave Mistake
Spell Found
Fatal Fortune

LEXY BAKER (COZY MYSTERY SERIES)
Lexy Baker Cozy Mystery Series Boxed Set Vol 1 (Books 1–4)

Or buy the books separately:

Killer Cupcakes
Dying for Danish

Murder, Money and Marzipan
3 Bodies and a Biscotti
Brownies, Bodies and Bad Guys
Bake, Battle and Roll
Wedded Blintz
Scones, Skulls & Scams
Ice Cream Murder
Mummified Meringues
Brutal Brulee (Novella)
No Scone Unturned
Cream Puff Killer
Never Say Pie

KATE DIAMOND MYSTERY ADVENTURES
Hidden Agemda (Book 1)
Ancient Hiss Story (Book 2)
Heist Society (Book 3)

SILVER HOLLOW (PARANORMAL COZY MYSTERY SERIES)
A Spell of Trouble (Book 1)
Spell Disaster (Book 2)
Nothing to Croak About (Book 3)
Cry Wolf (Book 4)

MOOSEAMUCK ISLAND (COZY MYSTERY SERIES)
A Zen for Murder
A Crabby Killer
A Treacherous Treasure

HAZEL MARTIN (HISTORICAL MYSTERY SERIES)
Murder at Lowry House (Book 1)
Murder by Misunderstanding (Book 2)

LEIGHANN DOBBS

A Purrfect Alibi

bookouture

Published by Bookouture in 2019

An imprint of Storyfire Ltd.
Carmelite House
50 Victoria Embankment
London EC4Y 0DZ

www.bookouture.com

ISBN: 978-1-83888-106-1
eBook ISBN: 978-1-83888-105-4

Chapter One

It's not every day that the guesthouse you own is filled with tarot readers, crystal-ball gazers and psychic mediums, so one needs to take advantage of that when it happens. Which is how I found myself seated at a small antique mahogany table in the parlor across from Madame Zenda, who was laying out a row of colorful tarot cards.

"That's a lovely card, look at those reds and the blues!" Millie Sullivan, my mother's best friend and the woman I had bought the Oyster Cove Guesthouse from, leaned over my shoulder and pointed at a card that depicted a dashing knight on a horse waving a sword. Millie had sold me the old mansion, which was badly in need of repairs, because she wanted to retire. To "get out and do things". Things that, so far, mostly consisted of getting into trouble alongside my mother. But the truth was, since I'd taken ownership, it seemed as if they'd both been here more than when Millie had owned the place.

Madame Zenda tapped the card with a sausage-like finger. She had to be in her late seventies, and was thin as a rail, with a face like a bloodhound and large, meaty hands. "A restless mind or a sudden surprise."

"See, I told you that you should ask Mike to the Marinara Mariner for dinner on Wednesday." Millie poked me in the shoulder. "They have a chicken-parm special that is out of this world. That might calm your restless mind."

"Wait." My mother, who was standing over my other shoulder, piped up. "Maybe the sudden surprise is that Mike is going to

ask *her* out. I think Josie should hold off. You know, play hard
to get. Men always want what they can't have."

"Don't I know it." Millie's voice carried an air of authority.

I sighed but remained silent.

Mike was Millie's nephew and also the town building inspector.
I'd known him since I was a kid when he'd been my brother's best
friend. I guess you could say we sort of had a history. Nothing
too sordid, so don't get your hopes up. That had been a long
time ago, though, and much water had passed under that bridge.
Mom and Millie had been trying to push us together ever since
I'd moved back to town, but I wasn't in the market. One of the
reasons I'd moved back to my hometown of Oyster Cove was
that I'd recently gone through an unpleasant divorce. I had no
intention of repeating that mistake any time soon.

Across from me, Madame Zenda was making a big show of
selecting the next card, her gold bracelets jangling as she waved her
hairy arms over the deck she held in her hand. She was wearing
some sort of flowing caftan with vibrant reds, purples, and oranges
that matched the cards she laid out. Her curly gray hair bobbed
around her head like unruly springs. She flipped the card.

Millie gasped.

I looked down at the card; a skeleton in armor riding a horse.

Madame Zenda stared at the card, her bushy gray eyebrows
mashing together like two elderly caterpillars jostling for the best
spot on a leaf. Her hazel eyes clouded over. "Is that a skeleton?"
Mom asked.

Millie leaned closer to the table. "That can't be good."

"It's the death card," Madame Zenda said softly, then hastened
to add, "but it doesn't always mean death."

"Well if it does, you're too late," Millie said. "There's already
been a death here a few weeks ago."

"And a few weeks before that, too," my mother added.

"You've had several deaths here recently?" The question came from another of my guests, Victor Merino. He had been sitting cross-legged in the mahogany-trimmed upholstered chair in the corner, his eyes closed, hands on his knees, palms up. He was wearing a royal-blue velvet sweatsuit and had a shaggy, oversized mustache. I wished he wouldn't sit like that on the chair, it was a delicate antique. He claimed he talked to dead people and apparently our talk of dead bodies had roused him from his meditation. I can't say I was sorry about that, his constant *ohm*-ing was starting to drive me up the wall.

"Oh, nothing to do with the accommodations here at the guesthouse," Millie added quickly. "You are in no danger. Those folks had it coming to them. Err... I mean, someone had a grudge against them."

"Yeah, and don't think it was Josie's cooking either," Mom said. "She's getting a lot better."

Meow! Nero, a black-and-white tuxedo cat that had come with my purchase of the guesthouse, hopped up onto the windowsill and fixed my mother with a slit-eyed gaze. I nodded at him approvingly. At least someone was sticking up for my cooking. I mean, that little incident when I practically burned down the guesthouse with my overcooked banana loaf was just one teeny mistake. I'd been whipping up some fine breakfasts lately, even if I did say so myself. Sunlight spilled in from the window highlighting Nero's glossy, jet-black fur. His intelligent golden eyes met mine and then he glanced out the window. Following his gaze, I caught a flash of something pink. *What was that?*

I leaned over to look outside. "Did you see that?"

"What?" My mother glanced out as Marlowe, the other guesthouse cat, hopped up to join Nero. She settled in next to Nero, her black-and-orange tortie-patterned fur mingling with his jet black. I went to get a better look. The window was cracked open and I could smell the ocean breeze and hear the far-away call of the gulls. The guesthouse sat atop a hill with a sweeping view of Oyster Cove, but not from the front parlor. From here all I could see was the long driveway and part of the overgrown gardens. *Wait… was that movement?* I could have sworn I saw someone moving around in the thick shrubbery, but who would be lurking outside?

"I don't see anything," Mom said.

"Me neither." Victor had come over to look out. "Let's get back to these dead people. You say there have been several deaths here over the past few weeks?"

Millie turned to face him. "Yes, but let's not dwell on that. I mean, it could happen anywhere."

Mom nodded. "That's right. When a person is determined to kill someone, the location is hardly a consideration. Just because it happened here shouldn't be a concern."

"Oh, I'm not concerned," Victor said. "I'm intrigued. Their spirits may still be around, and it would be good practice to talk to them. Might help me get a line on old Jedediah Biddeford."

Getting a "line" on old Jedediah Biddeford was the reason my guesthouse was filled with psychics. A few weeks ago, his skeleton had been found inside the wall during renovations. Turned out someone had put him in there about three hundred years ago. So, I guess there had actually been three murders at the Oyster Cove Guesthouse. Well, three that we knew about, anyway. Jed had been a seafaring merchant back in the day and had set off for Europe to bring back treasure. He'd never returned. Or, so they'd thought. Turns out he *had* returned and someone had killed him and closed him up inside the wall. No one knew what had happened to the treasure. Was it buried here on the grounds or had the killer taken it? My bet was on the latter, but these psychics had all come to try to communicate with his ghost so they could find the treasure.

I doubted there actually was any treasure, but they were paying guests and I needed the money. I'd spent my life savings on buying the guesthouse and had recently taken out a substantial loan to get the renovations done. I wasn't about to turn away guests, even if they did think they could chat with someone who had been dead for three hundred years. I just hoped they wouldn't kill each other in the process. Judging by the level of animosity between them, I would have to keep a close eye out.

"You *do* need the help communicating, Victor," Madame Zenda muttered. See what I mean? These folks had history and were constantly sniping at each other.

"Look who's talking." Victor waved at the tarot cards. "Your readings are never anywhere near accurate. Predicting something that happened weeks ago."

"You should talk." Gail Weathers stood in the doorway cupping a mug of tea in her hands. Gail was a short, stout woman with long, snow-white hair. She was a tea-leaf reader and had just about depleted my stock of Earl Grey. Millie was partial to her because she'd read her tea leaves and told Millie she would soon find love and fortune. "Last week you were called out for researching your audience in advance of the show you did in Boston."

"I like to know who is in the audience. I wasn't cheating; those dead folks really did come through for their loved ones." Victor crossed his arms over his chest and stepped toward Gail. "At least I can read *something*. Those tea leaves of yours are useless. What a scam. You can't be very good if I've never heard of you, I've worked with the best in the business."

Gail glared at him as she proceeded to the sofa, carefully holding her mug.

"People! Stop arguing." Esther Hill, a pleasant little old lady with sparkling blue eyes, got to her feet from where she'd been seated at a small, square, oak table near a window. The table had been set up with a black velvet cloth upon which sat a luminous crystal ball. If you ask me, she was the nicest of the bunch. Unlike the others, she was dressed normally in a powder-blue cardigan and navy slacks. "If you want a reading, Josie, come over here. I have much to tell you."

She motioned me to the chair across the table from her and we both sat. In between us the crystal ball winked ominously. I wondered if it, too, would reveal death. *Mew.*

Nero hopped up on the table and gazed into the ball as if he was wondering the same thing. Esther smiled down at Nero and petted the top of his head. Nero purred and looked at her adoringly. I scowled. The cats never looked at me that way. I was still getting used to being owned by cats. Yes, you heard me correctly. Since I'd come to the guesthouse, I'd learned that one didn't own cats, it was the other way around. Though my relationship with Nero and Marlowe had improved vastly since that first day, I still had a lot to learn. Esther waved her hands over the crystal ball. Unlike Madame Zenda, she didn't have a lot of jangly bracelets or loose-flowing sleeves, but her technique was just as impressive. She bent her neck to peer closer into the ball. I did the same. Nero did too. Esther was making a lot of faces. I wasn't sure what she was seeing; all I saw was my own reflection, except upside down.

"Aha!" She lifted her head, a mischievous smile on her face. "I see something in your future."

"What is it?" Hopefully not a dead body.

Her smile widened. "Someone tall, dark and handsome."

"We know who that is!" my mother said.

"That's right. Mike. I told you you should ask him out," Millie added.

"See? My reading wasn't off," Madame Zenda said from the corner where she'd been pouting.

"I saw that in the tea leaves!" Gail piped in from the sofa.

"Lots of men are tall, dark and handsome," I said. Though Mike really was tall, dark and handsome. Still, it was the cliché crystal-ball reading and I wasn't putting much weight into it.

Thunk!

We all jerked our attention in the direction of the mantle where a small candlestick had fallen on the floor.

"Where did that come from?" Gail asked.

"That looks like Great-grandma Sullivan's brass beehive candlestick." Millie bustled over and picked up the stick, then placed it back on the mantle. "It must've been right on the edge. Maybe Flora moved it too close when she was dusting."

I was skeptical about that because I wasn't sure Flora actually dusted the mantle. Flora had been the maid at the Oyster Cove Guesthouse since Millie was a child. No one really knew how old Flora was, but one thing I did know was that she was the world's worst maid. Almost every chore I asked her to do was met with an excuse as to why she couldn't, or wouldn't, do it. But Millie had been pretty insistent that I keep Flora on. She'd explained that the elderly maid didn't have much in social-security income. She depended on the wages here and she'd been very loyal to Millie's family. No one else had applied for the job, so I'd kept her. Anyway, I shouldn't complain—she had come through for us during the apprehension of the latest killer, so I guess I should give her a pass on the dusting and, I had to admit, I was getting sort of attached to her.

"I didn't put anything close to the edge." As if summoned by her name, Flora appeared in the doorway. She was a tiny thing, about four feet tall, with wisps of cotton-white hair sticking up and gigantic round glasses that gave her eyes an owlish appearance. Apparently, her hearing wasn't as bad as her eyesight. Her eyes fell on the crystal ball and grew even bigger, if that was at all possible. "Oh, you giving readings?" Flora sidled over to the table.

Esther smiled and gestured to the chair I was currently occupying. "Won't you sit down?"

Apparently, my reading was over, so I stood up. Say what you will about me, but I can take a hint. Esther produced a card seemingly out of nowhere and pressed it into my palm. "In case you want to recommend me to a friend."

Flora dropped the feather duster she had in her hand on the table and sat in the chair. Esther went into her hand-waving and crystal-ball-peering act.

"Aha!" She looked up sharply at Flora.

Flora frowned. "What?"

"I see someone special in your future."

Flora straightened and smiled. "Someone tall, dark and handsome?"

Esther shook her head. "No. Small, pink and wrinkly."

Flora made a disgusted face and waved her hand. "Oh, that's Harold Ditmeyer. I already dated him last month."

Esther looked at her funny. "I wasn't talking about a man. I was talking about a baby. You're going to have another great-grandchild."

Flora looked disappointed. "Oh darn. I already have dozens of those. I was hoping to get a good reading like Josie got."

Esther nodded. "Sorry. I can only convey what the ball shows me."

"Sure." Victor had been leaning against the mantle. Probably so he could look down his nose at all of us, which he was doing now to Esther. "Like that crystal ball shows you anything."

Esther glared at him, her normally kind eyes turning hard. I thought she was going to really lay into him, but she simply took a deep breath and said in an even voice, "Victor, you're not the only one who has gifts."

"Yeah," Madame Zenda said. "You have no respect for anyone."

"That's right." Gail stood, still cradling the mug. "Why, I have a good mind to—"

"Oh look, someone's here!" Millie pointed out the window. Even though I knew she was doing it as a distraction to keep the guests from descending into another argument, I rushed to the window remembering the flash of pink I thought I'd seen earlier.

It wasn't a person she had seen though. It was a car. My spirits sank when I saw whose car it was. Myron Remington.

"Is that the tall, dark and handsome man I saw in the crystal ball?" Esther asked.

"I should say not," I replied. Myron was neither tall, dark, nor handsome. He was short, stout and annoying. Ever since he'd offered to give me a low-interest loan for some badly needed repairs he'd been acting as if the guesthouse was his pet project and stopping by periodically to check on his little investment. I guess he had a fondness for the place. Myron's family went back as far as the Biddefords and his ancestors had even worked for Jed. That's why he wanted to make sure I had the funds to restore the guesthouse to its previous glory. He claimed he was proud of his family's modest roots in the community and wanted to show that he took pride in that by loaning the money to restore one of the oldest properties in town.

Mom and Millie insisted it was because Myron had a crush on me. Either way, I had to play nice with him because I'd already invested the very last penny I had in pre-ordering all the lumber and supplies so I could get a bulk discount. I needed to stay on Myron's good side—that loan was critical to my success.

I glanced up at Mom and Millie who had smirks on their faces. I narrowed my eyes at them to discourage any chatter about a romance between Myron and myself and headed to the front door. As I left the room, I looked back toward Madame Zenda. She was seated at the table, looking over the cards she'd laid out earlier. A breeze gusted in from the window, sending the cards scattering and my thoughts drifting to the death card. I didn't particularly care for Victor, but I had to admit that I hoped he was right in thinking Madame Zenda's reading was off. Because if the death card didn't represent the deaths that had already happened, then what did it represent?

Chapter Two

The front door to the guesthouse was unlocked during the day. It was mostly so guests could come and go, but I figured if a wayward tourist wandered in and booked a room, all the better. Myron had let himself in and was already standing in the foyer when I got there. He was wearing a designer suit and silk tie as usual. His face brightened when he saw me and I squelched the urge to make a face. I wouldn't go as far as to go out on a date with him or anything, but remaining friendly seemed the best course for the continued flow of finances.

"How nice to see you, Myron. What brings you here today?" I asked.

Myron adjusted the cuffs of his jacket. "I was just coming to check on my little project. Need to keep the investments of the bank in mind, you know."

"Of course." I started down the hallway toward the west wing where the current renovations were taking place. Myron followed. I could hear his shoes squeak to a stop at the doorway to the parlor and I turned to see him peering in, a frown on his face.

I backtracked to see what had him frowning. I suppose the scene was a little odd. Mom and Millie were clustered around Esther who was waving over the crystal ball again. Victor had gone back to meditating, this time in the middle of the room. Madame Zenda was practicing some kind of fancy shuffling maneuver, her bracelets clanging and sleeves flowing. Gail had laid down on the sofa and appeared to be napping. Nero and Marlowe trotted over and started sniffing Myron's shoes.

"What is going on here? What kind of guests are you entertaining?" Myron asked.

"They're psychics," Flora said. She was standing next to the grand staircase dusting the shade of a Tiffany stained-glass lamp that sat on a small table.

"Psychics?" Myron pursed his lips as if to indicate he took a dim view of psychics. "Is there some kind of convention?"

"Nope. They're trying to talk to Jedediah Biddeford. Gonna dig up the treasure." Flora kept her focus on the shade even though she was talking to Myron.

"You don't say." Myron glanced at me. "You don't really believe that, do you?"

I didn't, but I didn't want to say that in front of the guests who were now all looking at us. "You never know."

"I thought it was determined that there was *no* treasure," Myron said.

"Correction." Victor had been roused from his meditation and was now standing in the doorway. "No treasure was ever *found*. I aim to find it as well as uncover who really killed Jedediah Biddeford."

Myron looked skeptical. "The police couldn't even figure that one out, but good luck to you."

"You'll see."

Victor sounded as if he was getting ready for an argument, so I gave Myron's arm a little tug. I hope he didn't get the wrong idea.

"I think you'll be happy with the progress on the renovations." I gestured for Myron to precede me down the hall. Thankfully he took the hint and started walking. "I hope so." He whipped out a small notepad and a lovely bone-colored pen with carvings all around it. Was he going to write me up if my renovations weren't up to snuff?

I led Myron down the hallway to the west wing. That's where I was doing most of the renovations. It had once been a sumptuous ballroom, but since the days of balls were long over I was turning it into a game room.

Ed O'Hara, the elderly carpenter I'd hired to do the renovations, was skim-coating the joints on the sheet rock covering the wall inside of which we'd discovered Jedediah Biddeford's skeleton.

"Great, I see there's no evidence of what happened here before." Myron crouched down, his face inches from the wall and then put the paper and pen down on the floor so he could run his fingers along the joint. "That's good, no sense in scaring future guests off by making it obvious that there was a skeleton in the wall."

Even before he'd lent me the money, Myron had been a bit disturbed that we'd uncovered the skeleton. But now that I'd taken out the loan, he seemed to be getting kind of bossy about the whole thing. I get that he had an interest in the cash flow of the Oyster Cove Guesthouse and my ability to make payments, but I didn't want him telling me what to do with my business. Then again, maybe his constant trips over to check up on progress really were about his having a crush on me. I shuddered to think of it. Myron definitely was not my type. Ed met my gaze over Myron's head and rolled his eyes. I liked Ed, and even though he'd been spending a lot of time in my kitchen eating when he should be working, he was still worth the money I paid. I also felt a little guilty that he'd been one of my suspects during the most recent murder and I was trying to make up for that by giving him extra baked goods. Those that were edible, I mean. I could tell that Ed saw right through Myron but knew enough to be patient and play along with his twenty questions.

"I got it all patched up now like nothing ever happened," Ed said. "In fact, I have an appointment with the building inspector in five minutes to inspect it and make sure we can move on to the next stage."

Oh, no… Mike was coming too? The day was really going downhill and it wasn't even noon yet.

"Well, hello, Sunshine." Mike Sullivan appeared in the doorway, smiling at me. Speak of the devil. I returned the smile. It wouldn't do to be inhospitable to the building inspector, and besides, Mike was kind of easy to smile at with his tall, broad frame and whiskey-hazel eyes.

Though I had to admit, it did irritate me when he called me Sunshine. That was a nickname he and my brother had given to me when I was younger and it wasn't as complimentary as it sounds. However, since I'd moved back to town, I'd learned to just ignore him when he used the nickname because whenever I got riled up about it, it caused him to use it even more.

"I'm here to inspect the wall. Myron, what brings you here?" His eyes flicked between me and Myron as if he thought I'd invited him. Mike was probably wondering why Myron was crouched on the floor.

"Just checking up on my investment." Myron stood and made a show of brushing off his slacks. "Now, Josie, I don't know about these psychics and all this talk about speaking to Jedediah's ghost. Maybe it's not a good idea to encourage that sort of thing. Rumors could get out about the guesthouse being haunted and that might affect bookings."

"You mean it might affect her ability to repay your loan," Ed said bluntly.

"I'm only thinking of Josie's best interests," Myron said.

"I didn't have anyone else booking the rooms and I figured there was no harm in it. Maybe they actually will dig up the treasure and solve the mystery." Did these guys think I needed them to look out for me? I could take care of myself and decide who to book as a guest in my own guesthouse.

"Treasure? Mystery?" Mike asked. "Is that why Anita Pendragon is lurking around outside?"

My eyes jerked to the window. Is that who I'd seen fluttering around out there? Anita was a reporter who worked for the *Oyster Cove Gazette*. She was always looking for the "big scoop" that would make her famous. I'm sure it was no secret that I had a guesthouse full of mediums who wanted to talk to Jed's ghost. Maybe she'd smelled her big break and was spying on us to see what was going on.

"She was outside?" I asked.

"Yeah, I caught her taking pictures through the window." Ed nodded toward the big window on the east side. "I shut the shade. Wouldn't be surprised if she snuck in here though. I heard someone up on the third flooring where those old servants' rooms are near the attic, but when I went up to look no one was there."

Thunk!

A hammer landed on the floor beside Ed's toolbox. Ed picked it up. "Huh, that's weird. Guess I didn't set that squarely down on the box. Good thing we don't have those oak floors in yet, might have made a mark. I'll be more careful in the future."

Myron was peering out the window, hands cupped over his eyes, looking for Anita presumably. "If Pendragon gets word about this kooky plan to find the Biddeford treasure, she'll blab it all over. You have to do something about this, Josie."

"What do you want me to do? Kick them out? Have Anita arrested for trespassing?" I know I said I was trying to play nice with Myron, but I just didn't like the idea of anyone telling me what to do. "They'll only be here for a few more days. I'm sure it's all harmless. You don't really believe Jed's ghost is hanging around here waiting to talk to them after all this time, do you?"

Myron moved back from the window. I guess Anita wasn't out there after all. "I suppose not."

"Of course not. Hopefully they'll just try to communicate with him for a few days and then get bored and leave when he doesn't show up. No harm done," I said, ushering Myron toward the door. He could be a bit of a fussbudget and I didn't need him messing around with any of my bookings. I wasn't about to kick out paying customers, especially now that I really needed the money.

Mike and Ed started the inspection of the repairs Ed had done to date and I walked Myron back down the long hallway. The front door stood open, giving a nice view of the birch trees on the side of the driveway. We were almost at the front door when a loud clapping sounded from the parlor.

Myron pulled up short and looked in. Madame Zenda was standing next to the window, which had been pushed open even further. Was it stuffy in the guesthouse? I didn't think so— even though it was late summer—we did have air conditioning. And right now, most of it was going out the window. I made a mental note to tell the guests to keep the windows shut.

Madame Zenda clapped her hands again, pulling my attention from the window.

"People! People!" she yelled, leaning toward the window. "I have exciting news! Jedediah Biddeford has contacted me from beyond and he says he'll be giving me the answers to everything we seek tonight when the moon kisses the ocean."

The others murmured and looked at her skeptically. I could feel the disapproval radiating from Myron.

Madame Zenda continued, "After tonight, not only will I know where the treasure is, but also what happened to him three hundred years ago!"

Chapter Three

"When the moon kisses the ocean? What's that supposed to mean?" Marlowe asked half an hour later when she and Nero were catnapping in the conservatory. The conservatory had yet to be fully renovated, other than some replacement windows that Ed had put in as a surprise for Josie. That's why the cats liked it so much. No one ever went in there and there was always a pool of sun to lie in. The hand-carved trim that Ed had added around the windows as a surprise for Josie didn't hurt the ambiance any either. They could see Oyster Cove from an east-facing window and Nero enjoyed watching the lobster boats hauling in their catch, the waves crashing against the jagged rocks and the seagulls circling above. He didn't particularly like seagulls though, because they often dive-bombed the cats, but they were fine to watch from afar. He was glad to see the population was making a resurgence after an incident a few months ago that had caused a number of gull deaths.

Marlowe trotted over to one of the large potted plants Millie had brought over a few weeks ago and raked her claws through the dirt, then looked back at Nero for an answer to her question.

Nero sighed. "I've noticed these guests tend to be overly dramatic. I assume it was just a fancy way of saying when the moon comes up over the ocean."

They both glanced toward the window. The moon rose up in the east just around dusk. At this time of year, it was a glowing disk that loomed over the ocean highlighting the crests of the waves. It would be a full moon tonight. Nero wondered if Madame Zenda had chosen today to make her announcement because of that.

"They are a strange bunch," Marlowe continued. "I liked the last batch better. At least they had some cheese morsels in their rooms we could steal."

"These guests are sneaky, too. Though I do like Esther. She has no problem slipping us some treats under the table."

Marlowe, who had been examining the dirt inside the pot, glanced over at Nero. "Well, I wouldn't consider that any bonus. Some of Josie's breakfasts leave a bit to be desired."

"Yeah, but she can't screw up bacon."

"True. So, what do you make of Madame Zenda's proclamation? I noticed she made sure to be near the window." Marlowe finished her inspection of the plant and trotted over to the pool of sun.

"You mean the window she'd opened wider and let all the lovely cool air out of?" Nero plopped down beside her and started preening the white fur of his tuxedo. "I bet she was making sure that Anita Pendragon overheard her."

"That reporter that's been lurking around? Yeah, I could see her over in those gigantic overgrown rhododendrons and she looked pretty excited. I guess she doesn't realize that Madame Zenda was lying."

Both cats had a keen sense of the spirit world and they had sniffed the house thoroughly for signs of Jed's ghost when the skeleton had been discovered. There were no static disturbances, no other-worldly smells, no hint of ectoplasmic moisture. If Jed's ghost was still on the earthly plane, he wasn't hanging around in the Oyster Cove Guesthouse. Then again, Nero had noticed that items seemed to be falling to the floor at odd times recently and his hair had even stood on end inexplicably. But if a ghost were in the house, surely it would have made its presence known to them?

"Too bad she's going to end up being disappointed. As you know, there are no ghosts here for the humans to talk to. Had Jedediah's ghost been haunting this house we certainly would've heard from him by now."

"Boo!"

Nero nearly jumped out of his fur. He whirled around, back humped, fur standing on end.

A ghostly apparition floated next to the wall.

"Talk about being careful what you wish for." Marlowe seemed to take the specter all in her stride, calmly licking her front paw and rubbing it behind her ear.

"Jed?" Nero asked. In fact, he didn't really have to ask because he recognized the clothing from the skeleton they'd pulled out of the wall.

"One and the same," the ghost replied.

"So you really are here," Marlowe said. "I guess Madame Zenda wasn't lying."

"No. She was," Jed said. "I haven't talked to any of these kooks you have running around in here. She's making it up."

"Why would she do that?" Marlowe asked.

"Beats me." Jed swirled over to the window. "Nice view. I guess this room was added on after my time."

"There's been a lot of changes since then." Nero knew that the mansion had been much smaller in Jed's time. Over the years it had been expanded by his own descendants, as well as Millie's ancestors who had bought the house over a hundred years ago.

Jed nodded. "But it's not in very good shape." He looked kind of sad about that.

"So, where have you been?" Marlowe asked. "I mean, you've been dead for three hundred years, right?"

"I guess so."

"Then why pop up now? You weren't here a few weeks ago."

"I've been inside a wall, in case you didn't know. My spirit was just kind of hanging there in limbo. Only once my skeleton was freed was I able to roam about. It's taken me a while to get my bearings, though. I've been trying to communicate with you two but haven't been successful until now."

Nero nodded and watched as Jed floated about the room taking in the flooring, moldings, windows. Could Jed have communicated with Madame Zenda and not remembered? Perhaps she'd seen him floating around and was overly optimistic about their communication tonight. Or was she actually making that up, not knowing Jed's ghost really was around?

"So, you haven't communicated with anyone but us?"

"Nope. You're actually the first creatures that can see me. Guess my manifesting skills need work. I've been having fun messing with people though."

"Messing with them?" Marlowe asked.

"Yeah, I figured out how to push things off tables and such. I can't actually pick anything up, but the pushing off has been fun. Makes everyone jump."

Nero raised a brow at him. "Did you push the salt shaker off the counter the other day?"

Nero had thought he'd sensed something a couple of days ago when they'd been helping Josie prepare breakfast. He'd been up on the counter looking out the window, where he wasn't supposed to be, when his hair stood on end and suddenly the salt shaker slipped off the counter and smashed on the floor. Josie hadn't been happy about that and had scolded him.

"Yep," Jed said proudly.

"Thanks a lot. I got blamed for that." Nero was more upset that he hadn't known a ghost was present than getting in trouble with Josie. Then again, ghosts could be cagey and if their manifestation skills were lacking, it would be hard to sense them.

"Sorry about that." Jed really did look repentant. "Anyway, I've been spending most of my time in the attic. There's an area way in the back with a trunk that has some of my stuff in it. Feels kind of comforting and familiar, though I'm a little offended that it was shoved way in the back."

"A lot of people have lived here since your day," Marlowe said.

"I guess you're right." Jed looked around the room again. "Lots of changes. I'd like to see the old place get fixed up again. But on the other hand, I feel like I should move on to the nether regions. Wherever that is."

Nero nodded sagely. "The spiritual plane. It's where you will be most fulfilled."

"Whatever you say. Any idea how I get there?"

"Something must be holding you here," Nero said. "Say, do you know how you ended up inside the wall?"

"Nope. No idea. I just remember bringing my treasure back from Europe and next thing I knew it was darkness for three centuries."

"Wait! There really is treasure?" Marlowe's eyes glowed with excitement.

Jed nodded. "At least there *was*. Though it could be gone by now. As you said, a lot of time has gone by."

"And you were murdered," Nero said. That much had been obvious when they'd found the skeleton. If it hadn't been the crack in the skull that gave it away, it was the fact that a person couldn't very well wall themselves up from the inside. "The treasure could have been the reason, in which case you're right that it's long gone. But that could be your unresolved issue."

"You mean I can't move on until I figure out who killed me?"

Nero wasn't exactly sure about that. It seemed like that's what most ghosts who were stuck on this plane wanted, but he supposed each case was different. "It can't hurt."

"Too bad Madame Zenda really couldn't solve the murder, but even if she could talk to me, I wouldn't be able to tell her who killed me," Jed said.

"That's too bad. We'll have to figure out another way to find out who killed you." Nero loved a good investigation, even if the killer was long dead, but he had another motive for helping Jed. He didn't want the old ghost hanging around any longer than necessary. Lingering ghosts could be a nuisance and he liked things the way they were. He knew that as time went on and Jed got bored, his antics might not be as innocent as pushing things off tables. Best to help him move on to where he belonged.

"Yeah, but there's one good thing about Madame Zenda being a kook. It means that death card she pulled up is meaningless. That had me worried," Marlowe said. "But now that we know she's a fake, we won't have to worry about another death at the guesthouse."

Chapter Four

"You ask me, they're all a bunch of fakes," Millie whispered as she leaned against the door frame and peeked out into the hallway.

Mom nodded from her place at the table where she was eating a sliced-up apple. "Old and washed up."

"I did a little bit of research on them and I heard that Victor Merino was accused of fraud back in Ohio." Millie came back into the kitchen and rummaged in the new stainless-steel fridge. The Oyster Cove Guesthouse kitchen was a mixture of old and new. Old wooden cabinets painted a cheery yellow, golden pine floors so old that they were worn down in front of the sink and new appliances for cooking the delicious home-style breakfasts that the guesthouse had a reputation for.

Funny thing about the breakfasts; it turned out I wasn't much good at cooking them. That's why Millie kept coming over to help me out. I was learning, but I didn't mind Millie pitching in, it lightened my workload and kept Mom and Millie out of trouble. Right now, she was rummaging up some ground meat for a homemade turkey sausage recipe she'd pulled from her trusty stack of weathered and food-stained recipe cards.

"What kind of fraud?" Mom asked.

"A woman accused him of billing her thousands of dollars to communicate with her dead husband. Victor argued that he really was talking to the deceased and he had told her things no one else knew about. Her son claimed it was all information he got by reading old newspapers and asking around." Millie had opened a cabinet and was squinting up to the top shelf. Millie was only about five feet tall and I could see she had her eye on the old jadeite mixing bowl.

"Do you think any of them really can communicate with the dead?" I asked as I reached above Millie's head for the bowl and handed it to her.

Millie laughed. "I doubt it."

"Then why are they here?" Mom put her plate in the sink and ran some water over it.

Millie shrugged. "Who knows. Maybe they think Josie will pay them to talk to Jed. Or maybe they really are searching for treasure. Remember a few weeks ago when the whole town came out."

How could I forget? The discovery of Jed's skeleton last month had started a treasure hunt that involved most of the town. Never mind that legend had it that Jed had cursed anyone who stole his treasure, I guess people were more interested in money than they were afraid of whatever the curse might bring. "I hope they don't start digging, I just got the grass to green up over all the holes again."

"Why would Madame Zenda make a big announcement that Jed was going to talk to her?" Mom asked. "She seemed pretty sure of herself. Sounds to me like she really is going to talk to him. Maybe she isn't a fake."

I hoped she was. Images of the death card bubbled up again and I shuddered. "Maybe she figured if she announced it then the others would think she really was going to talk to him and give up?"

"It could be that. She's trying to stake a claim. Now the others have to come up with something better or more interesting. I think each one of them might be trying to get a sensational story to boost their careers." Millie cracked an egg and separated the white into a bowl. "I hear most of them have careers that are on a downswing."

My gaze flicked to the window. "Maybe that's why Anita Pendragon has been seen skulking around here."

"She has?" Millie stood on her tiptoes to look out the kitchen window. "Huh, I wonder if one of them called her so she could write a story on their supposed communication with Jed."

"Getting in the papers would definitely boost someone's career," Mom added. "And I did notice that when Madame Zenda made her pronouncement she made sure that her voice carried out the window. I thought maybe Jed's ghost was out there but now I wonder if she knew Anita was out there and wanted her to hear it."

"She was very loud about it." Millie whisked the egg white rapidly.

"Yeah, unfortunately Myron heard it too and he didn't look very pleased," Mom said.

I pulled out a chair and sat at the 1940s' Formica table, worry gnawing at my gut. "I know. He's worried that publicity about people talking to a ghost here could hurt the bookings at the guesthouse. What do you think?"

Mom made a face and looked at Millie, then bent down to pet Nero and Marlowe, who had trotted into the room and were sitting next to her looking at us as if listening to our conversation.

"Myron is a worrywart. I wouldn't worry about anything he says." Millie pulled a knife out of the rack and started chopping the onion and apple she'd laid out on the cutting board.

"Except if he really thinks that, maybe he won't give me the next installment on the loan. Or worse, demand I pay what I've borrowed in full. I already invested everything I have and without the loan the guesthouse will go under," I said. "Not to mention that I need the guesthouse to be fully booked to keep cash flowing."

Millie put the chopped apple and onion into a bowl, tossed in some sage and nutmeg and then plopped the ground turkey in and mixed it all together, then formed them into small patties and put them in the fry pan. Soon the sounds of sizzling meat and the spicy smell of sausage permeated the air. Millie flipped the sausages and then turned to face me.

"Myron is a man and he's easy enough to handle. I can tell he's sweet on you so all you have to do is dazzle him on a date and he'll give you the keys to the vault."

At my obvious look of distaste she continued, "You don't have to marry the guy, for crying out loud. But sometimes us businesswomen need to use every advantage. Lord knows I've had to many times." She patted the sides of her hair and smoothed her apron over her hips. I didn't dare ask for details.

Mom must have been still thinking about the treasure. "What I don't understand is how each one thinks they are going to get the treasure without the others seeing them."

Millie pursed her lips. "You know, that's a good question. I've noticed they're all following each other around."

I'd noticed that too. "It's like they don't trust each other."

"But if they are all fakes, then each would know the others can't talk to Jed," Mom said.

"Maybe they aren't sure about who is a fake and who isn't." Millie bent down to pet Marlowe who was doing figure eights around her ankles. "I know some of them have crossed paths before from what I read about them. Except Gail, she seems to have kept a low profile."

The cats had once been Millie's, but since she couldn't have pets at the senior housing complex where she lived, she'd made keeping the cats a stipulation for the sale of the guesthouse. At first, I hadn't been too sure, I'd never had a cat before, but I had to admit they were growing on me. As if sensing my thoughts, Marlowe turned her green gaze on me, eliciting all kinds of warm fuzzy feelings. Okay, I admit it, I was getting really attached to them, not to mention that they might have saved my bacon a few times in the previous murder investigations.

"Or maybe their whole goal is not to dig up the treasure or talk to Jed, but to get publicity?" Mom said.

Thud!

We jerked our heads in the direction of the sound to see a cookbook lying on the floor. The recipes, which had been torn from magazines and stuffed inside, spilled out. Millie walked over and bent down. "Here's that apple strudel recipe I was looking for!"

Mom glanced over at it. "Huh, guess Nero must've pushed that off."

Merow! Nero caterwauled from the other side of the room, then pranced over to the book, sniffed, looked up at the ceiling and started doing figure eights in front of the book.

Millie frowned down at him. "See, he ran over to the other side of the room and now he's pretending he didn't push the book off."

Meow! Nero's intelligent gaze flicked from Millie to me to a spot near the window.

Meow. Marlowe joined him in the pacing and gazing.

"Josie, I think they might be hungry." Millie gestured toward their empty bowls as she placed the recipes back in the book and put it in the bookcase.

Meeeeoww. Nero sounded exasperated, indicating that I'd better get those bowls filled right away before he started to make a racket.

Millie straightened. "Something's fishy about this Madame Zenda character. I think we need to set our sleuthing skills to determine what she's up to. I don't like anyone taking advantage of the legends here at the guesthouse for their own gain."

Millie's words set off my internal alarm bells. She and Mom were known to go a bit to the extreme and get into trouble. I didn't need them doing anything that would bother the guests and might result in a bad review on Yelp.

"Just how will you do that?"

Millie shrugged. "I suppose we'll do some stealth detecting and find out what her angle is. Maybe follow her and see if she really does communicate with Jed."

"Good idea." Mom pushed up from the table. "Let's go get our black outfits and we'll come back later tonight. Should we get our hair done?"

Millie patted the sides of her hair. "Might be a good idea. If we expose her as a fraud we might be on TV."

They started toward the door, and Millie threw a backward glance at the stove. "Josie don't forget to watch the sausage. Cook until they are no longer pink and then drain them on a paper towel."

"Will do." They left and I turned my attention to the cats. "I don't think this is going to end well."

Meewoo. I was pretty sure that was Nero's way of voicing his agreement.

Meooup. Marlowe chimed in.

I was glad they agreed with me, but the way they were still skulking around the bookcase instead of rushing to their food bowls made me uneasy. Typically food was their main priority. Then again, sometimes they delighted in doing the opposite of what I thought they would do, maybe this was one of those times.

Chapter Five

"See? I got in trouble for that cookbook." Nero glanced up at Jed. At least the ghost looked contrite. Some of them could be downright unrepentant about their mischievous antics, but Jed seemed to be a kind spirit. Even so, Nero still hoped he didn't hang around the guesthouse for any length of time.

"Sorry 'bout that, I was trying to get the attention of the pretty redhead."

"Josie?" Marlowe's eyes slanted as she looked up at the human.

Nero supposed Josie was kind of pretty. The coppery-red color of her hair was unusual and he liked that she didn't wear a lot of smelly makeup. Her greenish eyes, though not nearly as bright or luminescent as a cat's, were a good match for her fair coloring. He liked that she wasn't boney. Not that she was fat, but she had a bit of meat on her and Nero preferred his humans to have some padding because it made them more comfortable to lie on. But, best of all, she had a kind heart. Even if she was a little slow to catch on.

"I don't think you'll get her attention," Marlowe said. "She's not very advanced when it comes to communication with those other than her own kind."

"Well, to be fair, most humans can't see ghosts like we can," Nero said in defense of Josie. He'd been unsure about her when she'd first come to the guesthouse, but Millie had advised him to give her a chance and now he was starting to grow fond of her.

"True." Marlowe licked her paw and washed behind her ear. "What about our current guests? They all claim to be able to speak with spirits."

"So far none of them actually have," Jed said absently as his gaze flicked about the room. "Look at these new-fangled contraptions."

Nero glanced at Marlowe. New-fangled? While the stainless-steel appliances were a fairly recent upgrade, it was clear that Jed hadn't been keeping up with the times.

Josie opened the fridge and put the ingredients Millie had left on the counter away. The ghost's eyes practically popped out of his head. "Is that an icebox?"

"Yep." Nero swished his tail.

"Where's the ice?"

"Don't need any. Modern technology keeps it cold," Nero said.

"Go figure." Jed tore his eyes from the fridge. "I'm glad to see that people are taking care of the place, but it looks like Josie might be in a little over her head. The house still needs a lot of work. I sure wish I could help her out."

"Josie's working on it. Myron gave her a loan so she can speed things up," Nero said.

Jed's eyes narrowed. "Myron? Is that that fancy-dan guy who came over earlier?"

"Yeah, he thinks he's the cat's meow with his tailored suits, shiny cuff links and designer shoes," Marlowe said.

"Didn't much like him." Jed toyed with a delicate teacup that sat in a saucer on the kitchen table. It teetered in one direction then the other.

"Hey, don't shove that on the floor, it's from Millie's great-great-grandmother's Royal Albert china set," Nero said.

Jed snatched his hand away. "Sorry. Can't move it that far anyway. Try as I might I can only jiggle and wiggle things. I can shove them off if they are on the edge but that's about it. Maybe I just need more practice."

Nero hoped not. The last thing he wanted was for objects to fall to the floor repeatedly. Could be off-putting for the guests. Jed glanced at Josie wistfully. "I sure wish I could help her out."

If Nero wasn't mistaken, the ghost might be developing a crush on Josie. He'd seen that look before. Like one time when his feline friend Harry had a crush on that sleek white Persian with the blue eyes. He suppressed a sigh. Good thing Josie appeared incapable of seeing Jed. Ghost to human relationships never worked out.

Jed scratched his chin. "If that treasure is still out there, maybe we could get her to dig it up? She could use the money for the repairs on the guesthouse."

Marlowe's ears perked up. "You mean you might have some idea of where it is?"

"Well maybe, but…" Jed's voice trailed off.

"But what?" Marlowe asked.

"Well, I'm not sure, but I think my killer may have taken it. Or someone could have dug it up after all these years."

"Where did you bury it?" Nero asked.

Jed swirled over to the window. "Hard to tell after all these centuries. The land doesn't look the same. Judging by the view of the cove, seems like we're standing in the barn so I might have my landmarks mixed up. I'll have to look around out there—truth be told, I haven't been concerned about the treasure. Don't have a need for it now. I was more drawn to my old things in the attic. As a spirit, I find that haunting the most familiar places feels comforting. But if it can help Josie, maybe I'll widen my horizons and see if I can locate the area. Course if I do find it, I can't dig it up."

Nero flexed his claws. "How deep is it?"

"About two feet."

"We can probably bring Josie over and give her a hint," Marlowe said.

"That's *if* we can find it." Nero wasn't convinced the treasure was still there or that Jed would even remember the location. The grounds had changed a lot over the last several decades, never mind over several generations.

"I can't make any promises, but if I can find it, I might have an idea as to how we can get it dug up. First though, I need to go up and look the place over from the attic window to get my bearings. I'll be in touch."

And with that Jed disappeared leaving only a few drops of spirit dew on the floor.

"What do you think of his idea?" Marlowe asked, her gaze trained on the spot where Jed had just been as if trying to figure out how she could do a similar disappearing act.

"I don't know. It would be nice if Josie got the treasure, but I wouldn't hold my breath. If Jed even remembers where the treasure was, it will likely come to nothing. I think we should focus our energies on Madame Zenda's pronouncement. It seems to have disturbed the other guests and I sense foul play may be afoot."

Marlowe's ears perked up. "You don't say. I've noticed they are not a very trusting crew and I think some of them may be spying on the others."

"Indeed. And that Anita Pendragon hanging around does not bode well."

"Yes, I saw her lurking in the lilacs earlier this morning."

"Yesterday she was hiding in the hydrangeas." Beneath the hydrangeas was one of Nero's favorite napping spots and he'd been put out that he couldn't have his afternoon snooze because the nosey reporter was crouched down behind the bushes watching the house.

"And she was being furtive in the forsythia, too," Marlowe added. "I say we put a tail on her and see what she's up to."

Nero liked the way the young cat was thinking. As an older feline, he took his responsibilities to mentor Marlowe in the ways of cat detecting and human training very seriously.

"We need to follow all of them, something is fishy around here." Nero sniffed the air, the scent of salmon-flavored kibble causing his stomach to growl. Josie had finally left the kitchen after shooting a few concerned looks at their full bowls. Nero knew that she wanted them to eat and that, plus the fact that they'd been talking to Jed, had held him back from digging in. He didn't want Josie to think they would trot over and start eating at her command. But right now, she wasn't in the kitchen. "Let's eat first, though. We might need the energy to figure out what these humans are up to."

🐾

With the sausage all cooked and stored in the fridge for the next day's breakfast, I set to my cleaning tasks. Flora was dusting so I spent the next several hours doing laundry and vacuuming.

I couldn't help it if doing the tasks allowed me to sneak around the nooks and crannies of the guesthouse unobtrusively. It was part of my goal to make myself invisible so as not to disrupt anyone. I'd noticed with the last few batches of guests, being "invisible" allowed me to overhear some juicy stuff. I'd hoped to hear more about Madame Zenda's plan to talk to Jed's ghost, but today my guests were silent. Madame Zenda was in her room preparing for her ghostly meeting, according to Esther who I'd crossed paths with in the foyer. Esther had called an Uber and was on her way downtown. She was very tight-lipped when I asked her opinion about Madame Zenda's proclamation. She was also tight-lipped about why she was going into town, but maybe she just figured it was none of my business.

I was on my way to the back hallway to put the vacuum away when I spotted movement outside through the back parlor window. Anita Pendragon? Peering through the blinds I was surprised to see it was Victor Merino. He was skulking along the side of the house looking suspicious. Was he meeting with Anita? Trying to find a hiding place so he could follow Madame Zenda? He moved out of view and I scurried across the hallway to the butler's pantry. The window in there would allow me to spy on him without anyone seeing. Or so I thought. Someone else was already in there. Gail, who had her face pressed to the window, spun around looking guilty, which was good because if she was guilty then she wouldn't notice I'd been sneaking in here to spy on Victor.

"I was looking for some tea." She held up the ever-present mug as if to prove it.

"It's in the cabinet, same spot as always." I glanced out the window trying to see what she'd been looking at. I didn't see anything unusual unless you consider Victor tiptoeing through the overgrown gardens unusual.

"The tea leaves have told me to be aware of what's outside."

Something in her manner set me on edge. Now that I thought about it, Gail didn't seem to be a very good tea-leaf reader. Her readings were always very vague. At least Esther had come up with the tall, dark and handsome routine. And Madame Zenda had produced the death card. Madame Zenda claimed to be a medium, Esther could summon spirits in her crystal ball, Victor claimed he talked to those from the afterlife in his meditations, but, as far as I knew, Gail only read tea leaves. That seemed like a one-way conversation to me.

I pulled some Earl Grey out of the cabinet and handed it to her. Her gaze had drifted out the window again and she jerked her attention back to me and took the tin.

"I was wondering, how will you be able to communicate with Jed using just tea leaves?" I asked.

She looked confused. "What? Oh, well… the leaves don't actually help me talk to him directly. Not the way you think. But I see things in the leaves. Answers to questions. So I focus on a question and the answer is supplied."

I craned my neck to peer into her mug where a clump of crushed-up leaves sat on the bottom. It looked just like a regular bunch of tea leaves to me but who knew, maybe the arrangement of the leaves had some meaning for her. "Have you gotten any answers?"

"Unfortunately I haven't gotten anything from Jed." Her eyes were drawn back to the window as if magnets were attached.

"If Madame Zenda isn't full of hot air, he must be around. Maybe he doesn't like tea," I suggested.

"Maybe." Gail's gaze dropped to the tea mug and I sensed she had something to add but she remained silent.

"So what *have* you seen in the tea leaves?" I asked.

"Oh… A few things about the guesthouse. Nothing important."

"Things about the guesthouse? Like what?"

Gail's gaze dropped to the mug. "I see lots of renovations." She frowned. "And maybe some problems with completing them."

My left brow ticked up. You didn't need to be a psychic to see that I was doing a lot of renovations. "You don't say."

"Oh." She waved her hand dismissively. "I know you have renovations going on, but this is more than that." Then she glanced down again, a frown spreading on her face. "Of course, I also see something disturbing."

"Disturbing?" What could be more disturbing than a bunch of psychics trying to talk to the ghost of the guy I'd found inside the wall? I leaned over to look into the mug again.

Her face darkened further as Victor passed by the window, ducking and weaving in the shrubs. What was he doing? Trying to figure out Madame Zenda's location?

"Yes, you'd better be careful," she whispered, then tore her gaze from the window and forced a laugh. "Listen to me being all dark and ominous. Nothing bad is coming, just be careful around that Myron guy. And don't take what you hear from the guests too seriously. Everyone might not be on the up and up here." With that she raised her mug at me and turned to leave. "Thanks for the tea."

The conversation was a little unsettling, but I couldn't put my finger on why. I also didn't have time to think about it because two dark-clad figures lurking by the side of the house caught my attention. I pressed my face to the window. First Anita Pendragon, then Victor, and now this. How many people were skulking around in my yard and what did they want?

The two strangers resembled small, white-haired ninjas. Except they weren't strangers. It was Mom and Millie and they were heading for the kitchen door.

Chapter Six

I got to the kitchen just as Mom and Millie came through the door. They were wearing identical plain black T-shirts. Their white, spider-veined legs called for attention beneath the hems of their black shorts. I didn't have the heart to tell them that the white pompom-backed Peds and tennis shoes sort of ruined the look.

Millie went straight to the fridge, presumably to inspect the sausages. "Oh good, I see you browned them. Very nice."

"What do you think?" Mom gestured to the outfits. "We're going incognito tonight so we can find out what Madame Zenda is up to without being seen."

"It's not incognito, Rose," Millie said. "It's undercover."

"No, not really undercover… invisible, like a stealth bomber," Mom said.

Nero and Marlowe trotted in from the pantry and looked Mom and Millie over, then glanced at each other as if wondering what the two senior citizens were up to. *Mew.* Nero looked up at me. If a cat could roll its eyes, I swear he would have done it right then.

I noticed their bowls were empty. So, they *had* rushed over to scarf down their food as soon as I'd left the kitchen. They didn't fool me, I knew they liked to be ornery but I also knew they liked to eat.

"So you're going to hide in the bushes and follow Madame Zenda?" I asked.

"Yeah." Millie whipped out a copy of the *Farmers' Almanac*. "This here says the moon will rise in forty minutes. We better be on high alert."

Mom went to the kitchen window and cupped her hands around her eyes, peering out. It was dusk and the trees cast shadows in the dim light. In the distance, the ocean looked dark and ominous.

"We need to ascertain Madame Zenda's whereabouts." Mom sounded like she'd been brushing up on police lingo. Probably from one of the TV cop shows she and Millie liked to watch.

"Do you have an idea as to her whereabouts, Josie?" Millie asked.

"Last I knew she was in her room, but I really haven't been keeping tabs on her."

I knew Esther had come back and Victor was outside somewhere still. Gail had retreated to the back parlor with her tea. Had Madame Zenda already gone out to make her way to her meeting with Jed? Millie pressed her lips together and looked out the window. "I think we need to secure the perimeter."

"Where should we start?" Mom asked. "I mean, what's her most likely ETA and location."

"She mentioned the moon kissing the ocean," I said.

"Yes, but you can see that from anywhere," Millie said. "Most of the property has a view of the cove and I don't think she necessarily meant it would be in view. She was referring to the time she would meet with him."

"Funny thing," Mom said. "Why wouldn't she keep that a secret? It seems like she wouldn't want all the other psychics barging in on her meeting."

"That supports my theory that she is up to something. Probably wanted everyone to know." Millie nodded sagely. "Especially Anita Pendragon."

"So you're going with the theory that getting publicity about being the one who talked to Jed would boost her career?" I asked.

Millie nodded. "Yep, and she's lying about really being able to communicate with him."

Mom narrowed her eyes. "I don't like liars."

"Me neither, and that's why I want to catch her. If we can figure out where she is, then we can observe her and see if she is faking," Millie said.

"If we could figure out where she was going, we could get there ahead of time and stake the place out," Mom said.

"In our undercover outfits, we'll blend right in to the shadows." Millie looked thoughtful. "Did she give any clues as to where she might be meeting him?"

I thought back to her pronouncement. "No. She only mentioned the moon."

"True, but everyone knows that spirits like to haunt familiar places." Millie glanced around.

"Well that doesn't eliminate much. Wouldn't this whole place be familiar to him?" Mom asked.

"Not the *whole* place. Remember, most of this wasn't around in Jed's time." I turned to Millie. "Do you remember which sections existed back then?"

"Well, the main part of the house was in the west wing. And there were barns on the property that no longer exist. There is a part of the attic that I think has some old belongings of the Biddeford family and, of course, there is the three-seater."

"Three-seater?" I asked.

"The old outhouse. Three people could go at one time," Mom informed me.

"Well, if Jed's anything like my late husband, he'd be really familiar with that, maybe we should start there," Millie said.

"No. We have to think like Madame Zenda. What would she know about Jed?" Mom asked. "Everyone knows his skeleton was found in the wall in the ballroom, so maybe that's where she will go."

Millie shook her head. "That's not secluded enough. But didn't Ed say he heard someone on the third floor? He thought it might be Anita Pendragon, but maybe it was Madame Zenda scoping out a good place for her fake meeting. The attic would be ideal, and no one would know it was locked until they went up to check it."

I thought about Victor outside and Gail's frequent glances out the window. They'd probably been trying to figure out where Madame Zenda would go, same as Mom and Millie. "I don't think she'd do it in the house. I think all the others are trying to figure out where she is supposedly meeting Jed and the house is just too easy for them to find her. I saw Victor and Gail looking around outside. I'm not sure about Esther, she went into town, but she could have been waiting for Madame Zenda to get up from her nap so she could follow her."

"Well there's one place Madame Zenda might think would be familiar to Jed and it would make a perfectly eerie backdrop for her fake meeting," Millie said.

"Where's that?" Mom asked.

"The cemetery."

"But Jed isn't even buried there," I said.

There was an old family cemetery on the property and when Jed's skeleton had been found, his descendants had asked about burying him there but apparently it took an act of congress for that sort of thing to happen these days. And besides, the cemetery was overgrown and it would have been hard to even get the right equipment in there.

"Yeah but Madame Zenda might not know that. I'm certain she isn't speaking to his ghost and she is very dramatic. What better setting than the cemetery? It's creepy there," Mom pointed out.

Millie scrunched up her face. "I don't know. She might also be in the gazebo. That wasn't around in Jed's time but she might not know that either. You can see the cove from there and—"

"*Ahhhhhhh!*"

A blood-curdling scream split the air.

We jolted up from the table and ran towards the sound of the scream.

Chapter Seven

The scream had come from the northeast part of the property where the old family cemetery was. We dodged branches and fought through overgrown shrubs, my stomach sinking as we grew closer to the noise, which was now a low sobbing sound. Was it part of Madame Zenda's act or had something happened to her?

Millie reached the cemetery first and paused just inside the broken wrought-iron gate. The moon had risen, and the slab headstones cast eerie shadows on the scene. Something lay on the ground next to a triangular monument with a weeping willow etched on it. Anita Pendragon stood over it.

Anita looked at us, her mouth opening and closing like a fish out of water gasping for oxygen. She pointed at the body. Madame Zenda. Millie crouched down beside the body, which was no pretty sight. Madame Zenda had been stabbed in the chest. Blood soaked the front of her white caftan. The weapon looked familiar. I leaned closer and recognized the Oyster Bay Guesthouse logo on the handle. Anyone could have nabbed that at any time. But that wasn't the worst part of the scene. The worst part was the note on her chest that looked like it was written in blood. *Get out. Leave me alone.*

"What's that?" Mom bent down and jabbed her finger toward an old rusty buckle that lay beside the note. I was getting a little concerned that finding dead bodies didn't seem to faze my mother and Millie anymore. It wasn't such a big deal for me because I'd been going to school to be a medical examiner before my career was derailed with marriage and a daughter. I was used to seeing dead bodies and it wasn't just because this was the third one that had shown up at my guesthouse.

"Looks like an old buckle." Millie glanced up at Anita. "Did you kill her and leave this note and buckle?"

Anita's eyes widened. "No! I was following her to get a scoop on her talking to the ghost. But I lost her. I wandered around looking for her and then I stumbled upon that." She gestured toward the body.

Millie looked skeptical. "Did you see anyone else? Like the killer leaving the scene, perhaps?"

Anita's eyes darted around the area as if looking for the culprit. "No. It's so overgrown here, who could see anything? Besides, it's clear who the killer is."

"Is it?" Mom asked.

"Yes." Anita sniffled and let out a shaky breath before glancing around furtively and leaning toward us. "The ghost."

Was it my imagination or was Anita acting just a little *too* scared? It didn't escape me that the body and note would make a sensational story. And she *was* the only one here. Would someone else have had enough time to kill Madame Zenda, leave a note in her blood (if it was, indeed, in her blood) and an old buckle and scurry off before Anita discovered her? Had it really been Anita who screamed upon discovering the body or was it Madame Zenda's scream we'd heard as Anita was stabbing her? Anita was wearing a pink jacket and a white shirt underneath. Not a drop of blood was on her. Could she have changed clothes? She could have hidden another outfit anywhere in this messy overgrowth.

"I hardly think a ghost did this," Millie scoffed. "Where would he get the murder weapon? Or a buckle? Can ghosts write notes?"

"I've heard of ghosts doing lots of things." Anita gestured to the note. "And look at the note. It says to 'leave me alone'. All these psychics were bothering Jed. And what about that old buckle? It looks to be from his era. You ask me, that's a sign that it was him."

The buckle did look old, but I'd seen some very convincing replicas. A closer look would be nice, but I knew better than to disturb anything at a crime scene. Luckily, so did Mom and Millie. Despite Sheriff Chamberlain's crush on Millie, I didn't think he'd look too kindly on that.

A rustle in the bushes announced a new arrival.

"I called the police, they should be here any minute." Victor Merino appeared, giving the body only a cursory glance.

"How did you know the police would be needed here?" Millie asked. Clearly she was suspicious, and with good reason. Victor had hardly seemed surprised that Madame Zenda was dead. Was that because he already knew? He wouldn't be the first killer that doubled back to the scene of the crime.

"I heard the scream." Victor's eyes darted to the body again. I saw a flicker of something. Fear? Guilt? "I figured it couldn't be good, but I wouldn't have thought it was this. What happened?"

He was going to have to come up with something better than that to convince me. So someone screamed, so what? It could have been that someone saw a snake or a rat. How did he know the reason for the scream involved something that the police would be needed for?

More rustling in the bushes and Esther appeared. Unlike Victor, she was visibly shaken. Her hands flew to her face. "Oh my, how dreadful!"

Then she stepped a little closer, curiosity apparently overtaking her horror. "Is that a note?"

"Yes, the ghost left it," Anita said. She must have recovered from her grisly discovery because she'd whipped out her notebook and was taking notes.

"Poor Betty Sue," Esther said.

"Betty Sue?" I asked as everyone turned inquisitive eyes on her.

Esther nodded. "Oh yes, that was Madame Zenda's name before she changed it. Betty Sue Lipowitz. Did none of you know this?"

"No." How would we have known that? But the fact that Esther knew indicated a past relationship. They must not have been close friends though, because Esther didn't seem overly upset about her death. Millie zoned right in on that. "Did you know her well?"

Esther looked thoughtful. Was she reminiscing, or deciding how to cover up the nature of their relationship? Now that I thought about it, they hadn't seemed friendly at all, in fact they had seemed slightly adversarial. Then again, all the guests had seemed that way toward each other. I hadn't thought much about it as it seemed natural to have some professional rivalry in their business.

"Well, we weren't besties or anything but we've both been mediums for decades and have crossed paths before."

"Do you know why anyone would want to kill her?" Mom asked. By the tilt of her head and narrowing of her eyes, I could tell she had Esther at the top of her suspect list.

"Oh dear me, of course not. Such a shame. And what is with this note? Sounds ominous." Esther looked around, as if expecting Jed's ghost to appear from thin air.

"Yeah what is with the note?" Of all people, Myron had shown up. Now why in the world was he here? I thought about Mom and Millie's insistence that he had a crush on me, hopefully he wasn't stalking me or something.

He peered over at the body, his face turning visibly white. He looked as if he was going to throw up. "That looks like a warning." He turned his scowling gaze on me and visions of my loan drying up ran through my head. Dread curled in my stomach. Were Myron's concerns valid? I knew he was worried that rumors of murdering ghosts would affect bookings.

The sound of sirens split the air and Mom and Millie sprang into action, securing the crime scene as if they'd been deputized.

Millie moved everyone back from the body and Mom stood in front of them as if to provide a barrier. By the time Sheriff Seth Chamberlain and his deputies arrived on the scene things appeared quite orderly.

Seth glanced at the body, then at Mom and Millie, his gaze taking in their all-black outfits. He sighed and crossed his arms over his chest, then addressed Mom and Millie. "Okay, tell me what's going on? Who discovered the body and how did you all get on the scene? And what is with those outfits?"

Millie filled him in on what had transpired, glossing over the reason for their outfits and simply saying that they just happened to be both wearing all black today because it was supposed to be slimming.

"And see, right there is proof this was Jedediah's ghost." Anita snapped a picture of the note on the body with her cell phone.

"No pictures of the crime scene, please." Seth frowned at Anita. "And just what are *you* doing here anyway? You're not a guest at the hotel."

Anita shoved her phone back into her bag, making a show of rooting around. Was she avoiding eye contact with Seth? "I... uh... heard through the grapevine that Madame Zenda was going to contact Jedediah Biddeford's ghost. That's big news."

Through the grapevine? More like through my open window. But was that really the reason Anita was here? I could tell by the skeptical look on Seth Chamberlain's face he might be wondering the same thing. Did Anita and Madame Zenda have some sort of arrangement and if so, was Madame's death a benefit or a hindrance to Anita?

Seth glanced back at the body. "You don't really think a ghost did this, do you?"

"Well, sure, who else would do it?" Anita asked.

Good question. I looked at the group of people—Anita, Victor, Esther. Apparently, the scream had brought them out from the guesthouse just like it had brought Mom, Millie and me, but was one of them the killer? And why hadn't it summoned Gail? I would've been able to contemplate that more deeply if Myron wasn't standing beside me, wringing his hands and nattering on about having a bad feeling about this.

He leaned over and whispered in my ear. "This is not good for the guesthouse, you mark my words."

"Myron, what are you even doing here at this time of night?" I asked.

"I bet he came to ask you to dinner," Mom whispered.

Myron straightened, his cheeks flaming as if he'd overheard my mother and was embarrassed. "I came to check up on my investment. I heard Madame Zenda talking about her supposed meeting this evening and figured I'd better stop by and see for myself exactly what kinds of shenanigans were going on here. Guess it was a good thing I did." He let his gaze rest on Anita. "My suggestion is that you may want to get rid of those psychics right away. Bad publicity travels fast."

I wondered if that really was the reason, or if he had been about to ask me to dinner. Good thing none of us had an appetite anymore—hopefully the dead body would keep him from asking me out. Luckily, he didn't have a chance to because apparently something else traveled fast too—Myron's voice.

Seth snapped his head around and looked at Myron. "Get rid of them? I don't think so. Everyone here needs to be questioned." Seth waved his hand to indicate all the people who had gathered. "These folks are potential suspects. No one is allowed to leave town."

Nero stared at the body. The coppery smell of the blood made his whiskers twitch uncomfortably. He glanced sideways at Jed. "I thought you said you didn't talk to any of them."

Jed spread his hands out. "I didn't, I swear."

"Anita Pendragon seems pretty sure you're the killer," Marlowe said to Jed. The way that Jed was swirling and bobbing made it obvious that he was agitated. "Nah. Wasn't me. I can barely push a small item off a table. How could I stab someone? And why would I?"

Nero studied the ghost. He seemed sincere, but then again, ghosts could be wily. And Jed had disappeared abruptly during their previous conversation. Nero hadn't seen him since. He could have snuck out and murdered Madame Zenda and his claim that he could only push small objects could be a lie. Had he made a big show of it earlier just because he wanted an excuse as to why he couldn't be the killer? But why would he care about appearing innocent in front of the cats? He was beyond any punishment from the humans.

"What about the curse?" Marlowe asked. "Maybe you wanted to prove the curse was real."

"That was just hot air to keep people away. Besides, the curse was about someone messing with my treasure and I know the treasure wasn't here in the cemetery." Jed swirled over to inspect the body. It was obvious that none of the humans could see him. He passed by Victor and right in front of Esther. Anita shivered when he went right through her, but the others seemed oblivious. Of course, Nero couldn't tell if Madame Zenda could have seen him. She was beyond that. Maybe her ghost would pop up and enlighten them.

Jed's ghost bent down to inspect the note, then he hovered over the buckle. "No way I could do all this. I don't even write like that. That buckle does look familiar though. I think I might have had one like that on my going-to-church shoes."

"You mean that exact buckle or just one that looks like it?" Nero asked. Probably a replica. Because how would Jed's actual shoe buckle get on the body? Had someone been in the attic where Jed said his things were? Ed had mentioned he thought that he had heard someone up there, but as far as Nero knew the door was locked. Nero mentally added exploring the attic as the first item on his agenda for this investigation. It would be easy for him to get into the attic through the small crack in a door that led from one of the old servants' rooms on that floor.

Naturally, the cats would be doing a thorough investigation. Nero felt it was his duty to protect the guesthouse and Josie. As cat caretaker of the Oyster Cove Guesthouse, the responsibility to keep it running weighed heavy. Three murders in a row could be a major deterrent to guests.

"Why would someone want to kill Madame Zenda and leave this note if it wasn't you?" Marlowe looked up at Jed with intelligent, calculating eyes. Good, the young cat was also thinking along the lines of investigating and shared Nero's suspicions of the ghost.

"Beats me. Looks like someone wants them to think it was me. But why would I kill her? I don't stand to gain anything," Jed said.

Marlowe glanced at Nero and Nero nodded sagely as if he had some inner wisdom that validated Jed's words. He didn't but, since he was the mentor and Marlowe the mentee, he liked to put forth the appropriate impression of being wise.

"We'll investigate all options. But one thing is for sure. If it wasn't Jed, then we may have someone very dangerous on our hands." Nero glanced over at the body, where the police were busy photographing and cataloging, and made a mental note to be very careful around Jed. The ghost seemed sincere in his insistence that he wasn't the killer, but one could never be too careful. "Because whoever did this, definitely has a motive powerful enough to kill for."

Chapter Eight

"Maybe Madame Zenda was a little bit psychic after all," Millie said as we sat in the kitchen waiting for the police to finish with the crime scene.

"Why do you say that?" I asked.

"Well, she predicted a death in her tarot reading. Too bad it was her own death." Millie rummaged in the fridge, coming up with an apple, left over from the sausages, which she proceeded to crunch into.

"I don't buy that," Mom said. "If she was any good, she would have been able to see her own death and therefore avoid it."

Millie chewed the apple and glanced out the window. "Funny how Anita was already there when we got there."

"And how Esther, Myron and Victor showed up so soon after," Mom added.

"I guess the screams brought Esther and Victor to the scene, just like us," I said. "But I wonder why Gail didn't come running out."

Mom's brows shot up. "Maybe because she already knew what was out there."

Millie shook her head. "No, I think the most suspicious ones are Anita and Victor. And just what was Myron doing here, anyway?"

I filled them in on Myron's worries about all the ghost talk. "I think he's having second thoughts about investing in the guesthouse." I fiddled nervously with the silver salt-and-pepper shakers on the table.

"Don't worry about Myron, Josie." Millie patted me on the shoulder as if reading my mind. "He's all bark and no bite."

Mom nodded. "And besides, he has a crush on you. He's not gonna take the loan away."

"I know what will take your mind off of it." Millie rummaged in the cabinets. "We'll fix some nice lemon muffins for tomorrow's breakfast. They'll go fabulously with the sausage. What else are you going to make?"

I shrugged. I'd gotten so used to Millie coming over and helping I wasn't quite used to planning the breakfast. "Maybe some scrambled eggs? I'll heat up the sausage to go with it and then a fruit bowl."

"That sounds perfect. The muffins will round it out." Millie opened the fridge and gathered a lemon, eggs, milk and butter and placed them on the counter.

"So, we have another dead body and a slew of suspects. But I wonder… you don't think Jed's ghost really did kill Madame Zenda, do you?" Mom stood over at the bookshelf running her finger along the spines of the cookbooks. She stopped at the one that had fallen out onto the floor earlier.

Millie waved her hand. "Course not. There's no such thing as ghosts, right, Josie?"

"Right." I pulled out the new silicone muffin liners that Millie had suggested I splurge on and started lining them up on a pan. It would be convenient to think maybe Jed's ghost did kill Madame Zenda, but I didn't believe in ghosts. Someone more earthly had committed the murder and written that note. "But why leave the note and the buckle?"

"It certainly was dramatic," Mom said.

"*Overly* dramatic, but I suppose that was on purpose." Millie measured out the flour carefully.

"You mean someone is making it look like a bigger story than it is?" Mom said.

My thoughts raced to Anita Pendragon. Clearly Madame Zenda had known she was lurking around outside and wanted her to overhear the announcement about her meeting with Jed, but why was Anita lurking here in the first place? Had Madame Zenda tipped her off or had she just known psychics would be at the guesthouse and thought she could dig up a good story? What lengths would Anita go to to turn a good story into a *great* story? One can't be too hasty when trying to figure out a motive for murder though, and sprucing up a story so that it gets a lot of media attention wasn't the only reason I could think of to kill.

"The killer could also be trying to muddy the waters and use misdirection to distract us with the note and buckle, when the real reason for the murder is that it is about a past experience with Madame Zenda," I said.

"You mean like revenge or blackmail?" Mom's eyes lit up. "Esther did seem to know Madame Zenda from before. She must've been close to her in the past if she knew her real name was Betty Sue."

Millie turned to face us as she licked some batter off a spoon. "One of the last things Madame Zenda did was to make it very clear that she was going to talk to Jed's ghost. Seems logical to me that either someone didn't want her to talk to the ghost because he might tell her where the treasure is and she might get it first, or they didn't want her to get the fame that might come from an article. Unless the murderer is trying to make us think that is the motive, as Josie suggested."

"We can't rule out Anita Pendragon. She knew Madame Zenda was going to talk to the ghost and, according to her, she was skulking around trying to witness their communication. Maybe she figured out Madame Zenda was a fake and killed her to make the article more interesting," Mom said.

I was skeptical. "Would someone really kill over a newspaper article? I mean, it doesn't seem like that would be worth much. Too much risk for too little reward."

"But let's not forget, we must investigate all angles," Millie said. "Seems like there are quite a few motives for Madame Zenda's murder."

"Did you notice the murder weapon?" Mom avoided eye contact.

"Yes. My letter opener. But I keep that at the front desk and anyone could have taken it. The guests would have access and the front door is open during the day, so anyone could have come in and nabbed it," I said.

"Even Anita Pendragon," Millie added.

"Ed did say he thought she might have snuck in here," I said.

"Hmm, when did you last see it?" Mom asked.

I tried to remember the last time I'd seen the letter opener. I was sure it had been in the house last week but that didn't help. "I have no idea, with everything being electronic these days, I don't get much mail."

"It makes a good weapon, apparently," Mom said.

I crossed my arms and leaned back against the counter as Millie poured the batter into muffin liners. It wasn't a surprise that Millie and my mother were automatically jumping into a new investigation. What *was* a surprise was that I'd followed right along with them. Apparently investigating the last two murders had fostered some sort of detecting skill I didn't know I'd had.

Of course, the idea that a killer was running around loose wasn't very appealing. Nor was the idea that it could affect my bookings or my loan. Seth Chamberlain wasn't what I'd call a crack investigator. He did the best he could, but the town of Oyster Cove didn't normally have any murders and he just didn't have the experience. If Mom, Millie and I needed to do a little detecting on the side to catch a killer, then so be it.

"It's getting late. I think we need to sleep on it and come up with a game plan first thing tomorrow," Millie said as she shoved the muffins in the oven.

"I already have one. Or at least the start of one," Mom said.

Millie shut the oven door, straightened and turned to look at my mother. "What is it?"

"Someone went to a lot of trouble to dress up the murder scene. We don't know their exact purpose for that yet, but we do know one thing." Mom's eyes glittered with excitement. "Someone had to get an old buckle similar to what Jed would have worn. Do you remember seeing a buckle like that in here, Millie?"

Millie shook her head. "No. The stuff from Jed's time is way back in the attic and I've never looked in there. I suppose there could be such a buckle, but how would someone get it? You still keep the door locked, don't you, Josie?"

"I do. Can't have guests getting hurt up there."

Millie pressed her lips together. "Seems like a lot of trouble for someone to search the house."

"Yeah, there are easier ways to find old buckles or buckles that look like they are old," Mom said. "In fact, I think I've seen them at the fabric store."

"Ones that look like the one on the body?" Millie asked. "It would make more sense that someone just got a replica."

Mom frowned. "I don't remember exactly what they looked like, but it behooves us to go downtown and check it out. If we can find who recently acquired such a buckle, then we just may have our killer."

Chapter Nine

Nero and Marlowe had spent a restless night at the foot of Josie's bed. It was no easy task sleeping with a human. You had to be vigilant so you could judge the right time to inch your way up to the top of the bed and curl up around their nice warm heads while they were sleeping without getting swatted away too many times. And then there was the pressure of waking up early—a necessity if you wanted to lay on their chest and stare at them as they woke. Nero always got a kick out of Josie's wide-eyed reaction when her eyes fluttered open and she saw his face inches from hers.

While Josie was in the kitchen getting the breakfast ready for the guests, the cats did a cursory inspection of the rest of the house, which would be followed by their plan to search the attic. They found Flora in the dining room setting the table and they trotted in to rub against her saggy panty-hose covered legs to get their morning petting, before heading to the parlor where they could catch some rays from the morning sun.

To their dismay, the parlor was not unoccupied. Esther stood in front of the table where Madame Zenda's tarot cards were still laid out. She was studying the cards with a pensive look on her face.

"She reads cards too?" Marlowe asked.

"Maybe she's thinking about taking over now that Zenda is out of the picture," Nero said.

But Esther wasn't actually reading the cards. She picked them up one by one, placing them gently in a pile and then sighed as she put them off to the side. "Poor Betty Sue."

Noticing the cats' presence, her face cracked into a smile. She sat in the chair in front of her crystal ball and motioned for them to come to her.

"I don't think Esther can be the killer," Marlowe said as she trotted over and accepted a tuna-flavored treat that Esther had pulled out of her pocket. "She's nice and has delicious treats."

"Sometimes it's the nice ones that you have to watch out for." Nero felt it was prudent to exercise more caution in his assessments. He'd been around longer than Marlowe and had witnessed how humans often were not what they seemed.

Jed's ghost swirled into view. "Have you guys been up in the attic recently?"

"I caught a delicious mouse up there last week." Marlowe smacked her lips.

"Have you been way in the back where my stuff is? Who else goes up there?" Jed asked.

"As far as we know no one goes up there. That place is crammed full and it's hard to get around, for humans at least. I don't even think Josie has been through the whole attic yet," Marlowe said. "But we were just about to go up."

"Millie went up there when she was younger but, as far as I know, she hasn't been up there in decades. She's probably forgotten about everything up there as it is," Nero added. "It's all just a bunch of cast-offs and junk."

"Yeah well someone's been up there." Jed fisted his hands on his hips. "I took a look through the trunk with my things in it and my good dress shoes are missing."

Nero made a face and thought back to what the skeleton had had on for footwear. What was left of the clothing indicated that Jed hadn't been dressed up and Nero distinctly remembered the shoes didn't have fancy buckles like the one on Madame Zenda. "Well you *have* been dead for three hundred years. I suppose in that time someone could've gone up there and rearranged things. Or even borrowed your shoes."

Jed pursed his lips, apparently contemplating Nero's words. "I suppose. But the dress shoes that are missing had buckles similar to that found on the body."

This piqued Nero's interest. Their first clue! "You don't say? Maybe we better head up into the attic and see what we can find out."

"Yes, we need to figure out what is going on around here. I don't like that people are bandying about the idea that I could've killed that woman. I'm no killer. In fact, I was a murder victim myself," Jed said.

"Are you sure? You don't seem to remember things like where the treasure is." Marlowe slitted her eyes. "Maybe with your ghostly amnesia you don't know what you did last night. Have you blacked out or anything?"

"Certainly not. And I didn't forget where the treasure is. It's just that the landmarks have changed and I need to do some looking around to find the spot. I tell you, I'm no killer!" Jed's voice rose in outrage. "You ask me, it was one of these psychics. Probably jealous that Madame Zenda said she could talk to me."

Nero glanced sideways at Esther. She was gazing into her crystal ball intently, her kind face a study in concentration. Was she hiding something beneath that pleasant exterior? "Maybe we should do some investigating into each one of them."

"My money is on that blowhard, Victor," Jed said. "He's been running all around the estate trying to conjure me up with some lame chants and incantations."

"You haven't tried talking to him?" Marlowe asked.

"No. I haven't actually tried *too* hard to talk to any of them and even if I did, it wouldn't be Victor. I wouldn't give him the time of day." Jed glanced over at Esther and his face softened. "If

I was going to talk to anyone, it would be someone pretty. Like maybe that young filly over there."

Nero followed Jed's gaze. He wasn't sure what Jed was seeing but Nero only saw an old lady with white hair and a network of wrinkles. "Young?"

Jed laughed. "Well, I *am* three hundred years old, so she's young to me."

"Okay then, so back to the shoes. We'll go take a look. See if we can sniff out any nefarious human activity. But I don't think anyone has been to that part of the attic in decades." Nero wasn't sure if he wanted Jed to fixate on Esther. He was getting the same moon-eyed look that he got when he looked at Josie. Apparently the ghost was looking for love and Nero didn't want to encourage that. He wanted Jed to drift away to the afterlife and not linger in the guesthouse because he had a crush on some human. Then again, maybe if he set his intentions on Esther, he'd leave the guesthouse when she did and they could be done with him.

"I hope it was someone in this century." Jed's expression turned somber. "Though I suppose it could be the person who killed me—they were very expensive shoes. Or maybe it was my wife. She was mad that I went off to Europe for so long and there's no telling what kind of revenge she'd want to enact. Could have taken it out on my shoes."

Nero mulled this over. Could Jed's wife's vengeful ghost be lurking about in the guesthouse? The odds of two ghosts running around were practically nil, besides Nero's fine senses would have picked up on a second ghostly presence. It made more sense that the shoes had been taken a long time ago, which made them irrelevant to the current happenings. But then how did one explain the buckle?

"Are you sure that buckle was from your shoes?" Nero asked. "I mean, there must be plenty of similar buckles around."

"That one was old. Back in my day things were handmade so very few of the same thing existed. Sure looked like the buckle I had," Jed said.

"Too bad the police have taken it for evidence, otherwise I could try to sniff out the age," Marlowe said.

Nero's tail twitched in approval. The young cat was coming along nicely in figuring out how to use her superior senses to aid in their investigations. She did have a ways to go in knowing how to use their extensive network of feline detectives though.

Nero turned to her. "Good observation. But even if we cannot apply our noses to the buckle, we do have an informant who can."

Marlowe's green eyes widened. "Of course! Why didn't I think of that? We can ask Louie Two Paws!"

Louie was a polydactyl Siamese that hung around at the police station. He often came in handy when the cats wanted insider information on cases. Marlowe jumped down from the arm of the chair where she'd been perched and started out of the room. "Come on! Let's go downtown. We can visit Louie and consult with the gang first, then we'll check out the attic when we come back."

"The gang" was a group of cats that all helped to solve the various mysteries that cropped up around town. Unbeknownst to the humans, the cats had been doing this for decades. They wanted to keep the quaint ambiance of the town of Oyster Cove and having killers and thieves running around wouldn't do. Of course, the cats couldn't let on to the humans that they were the real masterminds behind solving the crimes, they had to make it look like it was all the humans' doing. It took a bit of cleverness to accomplish that, as humans could be rather dense when presented with clues, but Nero prided himself on the fact that they had a perfect record and no one suspected their involvement.

Nero was about to trot after Marlowe when he caught a whiff of spicy sausage. "We'll leave momentarily. But first, we might as well slip into the dining room and fortify ourselves with some sustenance. We'll need energy for the trip downtown. I'm sure Esther will slip us some treats and if we skulk along the edges and then hide under the tablecloths, Josie will never suspect we are in there."

Nero trotted off toward the dining room. His stomach growled in anticipation and he was only the slightest bit worried that he could be eager to accept treats from a cold-blooded killer.

Chapter Ten

Breakfast was a somewhat solemn affair. Esther, Victor and Gail sat together at one table. I hadn't seen them sit together before and didn't know if they were clustered together for comfort or to keep their enemies close, each being afraid the other had murdered Madame Zenda.

The smell of sausage and coffee lured me closer to the buffet server and I picked at a lemon muffin as I eavesdropped on their conversation.

"I just can't believe Madame Zenda was murdered right under our noses!" Gail wailed into her napkin.

"Speaking of which." Victor narrowed his gaze on her. "Where were you? That scream roused me out of a deep meditation. It was loud enough to wake the dead."

Gail sniffled and reached for her tea. She turned to Victor, a wan smile on her face, but not before I noticed a hint of malice in her eye. Was it simply that she didn't like the guy? I couldn't say I blamed her there, he was annoying. Or was she angry he called the fact she didn't come running last night to everyone's attention?

"I'm hard of hearing." Gail pointed to her right ear. "I drank some chamomile tea and was out like a light. With my hearing problems, I never heard a thing. When I got up, the police were here wanting to question everyone. Imagine my shock when I found out why."

Guess she hadn't seen the murder in her tea leaves. A movement under the table caught my eye and I tilted my head just in time to see a ginger-and-black tail disappear under the tablecloth. Marlowe. I was sure Nero wasn't far behind. Or probably in the lead. He seemed to be the instigator. I watched as Esther broke off a teeny piece of sausage and slipped it unobtrusively under the table.

There was no point in shooing the cats away. I didn't want to call attention to them in case the other guests hadn't noticed their presence. I'd also learned that telling them not to do something only made them do it more. Best to let them skulk around unnoticed. They seemed to be able to pick out the guests who didn't mind having cats in the dining room and were able to hide their presence from those who did, so there was no harm.

"You ask me, it could be that reporter. She discovered the body." Esther glanced out the window as if expecting to see Anita skulking around.

"But why would a reporter want to kill Madame Zenda?" Victor asked.

Esther shrugged. "Maybe Madame Zenda wouldn't give her an exclusive."

"Oh, did Anita ask you for an exclusive too?" Gail asked Esther.

Esther's eyes dropped to her plate and she got busy eating the rest of her breakfast. "Maybe."

Gail turned to Victor. "What about you? You've been awfully quiet with all your meditation. Did you talk to the reporter too?"

"I'm not quiet, I just don't associate much with beings on this earthly plane. I prefer to spend my time on spiritual endeavors. I'm perfectly happy to wait for Jedediah to contact me as I'm sure he intends to do," Victor said, avoiding the question.

Gail took a sip of tea, then looked down in the mug. Was she looking for something in the tea leaves? "But he was already going to talk to Madame Zenda. Why talk to the rest of us too?"

"Pffft… I doubt Biddeford's ghost was going to contact Madame Zenda, as she has no psychic talent. She was probably making that up for the benefit of the reporter. If such an article got picked up for syndication it could have helped her flagging career." Victor fluffed his napkin onto his lap with an exaggerated flourish. "You ask me, we should all be wary. There's a killer on the loose."

"I wouldn't be too sure that Madame Zenda didn't have any psychic talent. She did predict a death... too bad it was her own," Esther said, echoing Mom's words from last night.

Just then, the phone in the foyer shrilled. Darn it! I wouldn't be able to eavesdrop anymore.

I rushed to the foyer and plucked the wireless phone off its cradle. "Oyster Cove Guesthouse!" I chirped in my most pleasant tone. No need to sound somber as if a murder had just happened the day before, that wouldn't encourage potential guests to reserve rooms.

"Hi, this is Dolores Johnson."

I hesitated, the name was familiar.

The person on the other end continued, "I had a reservation for next week."

"Of course! Good to hear from you Mrs. Johnson. How can I help you?"

"Well, I hate to say it, but I have to cancel."

My spirits fell. "Cancel. But why?"

"Ummm... you see... we've decided to go somewhere else on vacation. I read on your website that you can cancel up to seventy-two hours in advance and get a refund, is that correct?"

"That's correct. So you're sure you want a refund? I can't guarantee the room will still be available if you change your mind again." The guesthouse wasn't fully booked, but you never knew when new reservations would come so it wasn't a total lie.

"Oh, I'm sure. Thank you."

I hung up the phone and stood there. Taking a vacation somewhere else? It was more likely word of the murdering ghost had gotten out. Maybe Myron was actually more perceptive than he let on. If news was spreading and people were afraid to come here, then I had to put a stop to it, and I knew of only one way—catch the real killer and then the newspapers would move on to more interesting stories.

I heard footsteps on the stairs and turned around to see Flora coming down. She had the big pink feather duster in her hand and was running it over the banister as she descended. She glanced down at me, the magnification of her large glasses exaggerated at that angle. "Something wrong?"

I sighed. "I just got a cancellation. I'm afraid all this ghost and murder business might be scaring people off."

"Darn, that's too bad." Flora swished the duster in the air and a shower of dust rained out of it. "I don't like that one bit. Of course, fewer guests mean less work for me but more guests mean job security and that's more important. Guess I was right in shooing that reporter off then."

"You mean Anita Pendragon? The one who has been hanging around outside?"

Flora descended so that we were at eye level, which meant that she was standing about four steps up. "Yeah, I caught her around the kitchen door looking like she was trying to get in."

"When was this?"

"Couple of nights ago. Though I shouldn't be surprised with all the goings-on around here. Tarot readings. Crystal balls. You ask me, all these people here are a bunch of weirdos. You should get a better clientele." She fluffed the air with her duster one more time, then shuffled off toward the front parlor muttering under her breath, "No wonder murders happen here so often."

I stood in the hallway a few minutes longer, thinking about what Flora had just told me about Anita. Why would she be trying to get in the back door and did that have anything to do with Madame Zenda's murder?

I didn't have a lot of time to think about it because just then I saw Millie's decades-old Dodge Dart drive in. Mom and Millie jumped out and hurried to the front door, stopping short when they saw me standing in the hallway.

"Oh good, you're ready," Millie said. "We're going down to Felicity's Fabrics. They have the largest selection of buckles in town."

I was momentarily confused. "Buckles?"

"Yeah, you know, like they found on the body." Mom lowered her voice. "If we figure out who bought the buckle, we figure out who the killer is."

"Speaking of which," Millie said. "Do you still have that book with the historical etchings and photos of the guesthouse in it? I think there might be one we can use to validate whether or not that buckle really is Jed's."

Millie had left lots of things in the guesthouse. Furniture, doilies, plates, glasses and books, including a history of Oyster Cove that featured historical photos, etchings and drawings of the guesthouse. It hadn't always been a guesthouse; initially it had been built by Jedediah Biddeford as a family estate, then over the years it had been expanded and eventually turned into an inn. I remembered one of the earlier etchings featured Jed and his family sitting in front of the house all dressed up. Apparently, Millie wanted to scrutinize it and see if we could match the buckle.

"It's in the kitchen."

Mom and Millie followed me into the kitchen where I plucked the book out of the bookshelf and handed it to Millie. Nero and Marlowe must have had their fill of breakfast treats because they trotted in and begged Millie for attention, which she had no trouble providing. After petting the cats for several minutes, she flipped through the book, stopping on the page with the drawing of Jed's family. Jed sat in a chair, a small child on his knee and older children beside him. A dour-looking woman in a voluminous black dress, who I assumed was his wife, stood behind him. Off to the side several servants were lined up.

Millie whipped out her cell phone and zoomed in on Jed's shoe. "Look at this! The artist must have been very good, it looks so realistic. Almost like a photo. And look at his shoes! Does this look like the buckle we found on the body?"

I peered over her shoulder. My memory of the buckle on the body was fuzzy, but it looked similar. "Hard to tell, that drawing might not be exactly accurate. Looks like it could be, but I'm sure the buckle on Madame Zenda wasn't an actual buckle from Jed."

"Yeah but why would someone go to the trouble of getting a buckle that looked like that?" Mom asked.

Millie snapped a photo. "Probably because they just wanted it to look like it could be Jed's. Maybe I can persuade Seth Chamberlain to tell me if the buckle is a replica or not."

Mom and I remained silent. Millie had a way of "persuading" Seth to tell her things about the investigation that he wouldn't normally tell a civilian. Neither one of us wanted to know exactly what she did to get that information.

"So far the only thing I've been able to get out of him is that the note wasn't real blood and the murder weapon was wiped clean." Millie shoved the cell phone into her large purse. "Come on, girls. All we need to do is show the picture of that buckle to Felicity and find out who bought a similar buckle and we can solve this case."

Chapter Eleven

Felicity's Fabrics was crammed with bolts of cloth—cotton, linen, taffeta, silk—in a rainbow of colors and patterns. Felicity, a woman in her sixties who had owned the store ever since I was a kid, sat at the register, her glasses perched on her nose and a colorful beaded eyeglass holder looped behind her neck.

"Millie! So good to see you again." She leaned across the counter. "Are you here for more sheer fabric for another nightgown?"

Mom and I glanced at Millie, who at least had the modesty to blush.

"No. I'm here with a question." She whipped out her phone and showed Felicity the picture of the buckle. "Do you have any buckles that look like this?"

Felicity pushed the glasses up her nose and scrunched up her face as she picked up the phone and held it at arm's length from her face. "This looks like an antique."

"Yes, but you have antique replicas here," Millie said.

"Not like this." Felicity handed the phone back to her.

"Are you sure? Has anyone been in asking about replicas of old buckles?" Millie persisted.

"Nope. Sorry."

"And you're absolutely sure?"

Felicity gestured to the side of the store where little cards hung in dozens of rows. "Look for yourself. These are all the buckles I have. You will find nothing that resembles the buckle on your phone."

Millie bustled off toward the buckles and Mom and I followed. I shot a "thank you" over my shoulder at Felicity. A few minutes of studying the buckles proved that Felicity was correct. Nothing even close to the buckle that had been on Madame Zenda's body was on display.

"Well, how do you like that, I thought we'd have this case solved by noon and could celebrate at the Marinara Mariner for lunch." Millie's shoulders slumped, the wind taken out of her sails.

Mom snapped her fingers. "Wait a minute. All is not lost. What about the antique store? I bet they have a lot of old buckles."

Felicity nodded. "Sure they do. Lots of old stuff over there. And Agnes is doing some restoration and repurposing work, maybe she restored your buckle."

We hustled toward the door, Millie stopping to admire a see-through pink polka-dot sheer fabric on display. I didn't even want to try to imagine what she would make out of it. Some things were just better not to think about.

Withington's Antique Store was across the street. Traffic was always light in Oyster Cove, so we sauntered across, admiring the colorful barrels of flowers and cheerful store awnings. The town had made sure that everything was in tip-top shape for the two hundred and fiftieth celebration a few weeks ago and the streets practically gleamed. Store windows sparkled; the cafe had put out several scrolly wrought-iron tables and chairs; and the whole thing was reminiscent of a Parisian sidewalk.

It was picturesque, especially with the cats that were trotting into the alley between the cafe and Withington's. Wait… that looked like Nero and Marlowe. As I watched, Nero glanced back over his shoulder, his eyes catching mine. I could have sworn he nodded before turning back and continuing on his way. This wasn't the first time I'd seen the cats downtown and it made me wonder how they even got down here. Was there some secret shortcut? If there was, I wouldn't mind finding out so I could use it myself.

Withington's Antiques smelled like old furniture and lemon pledge. It was crammed to the gills with oak servers, mahogany dining-room sets, crystal chandeliers and lighted glass cases full of vintage jewelry and knick-knacks. Agnes Withington had run the shop since I'd been in diapers and she had to be ninety years old. She sat behind the counter on a stool, a petite thing with a shrewd gaze.

She smiled as she recognized Mom and Millie. "Millie and Rose, what a pleasant surprise!" Her inquisitive gaze drifted to me.

Mom gestured to me. "Agnes, this is my daughter, Josie."

Her smile widened. "Of course, she looks just like you. I heard you came back and bought the Oyster Cove Guesthouse. Plenty happening up there since you took over."

You could say that again.

Millie whipped out her phone and slid it across the counter to Agnes. "Actually, that's why we're here. You might have heard there was an incident up there yesterday and we're looking for someone who would have purchased a buckle like this." Agnes squinted, then reached under the counter, producing a lighted magnifying glass, which she turned on to magnify the image on Millie's phone.

While she was squinting at it and moving the magnifying glass closer and further away, Mom drifted over to a display of beautiful old pens that sat at the end of the counter. They were fountain pens and each sat in a little holder, their golden nibs pointing toward the ceiling. "These are quite unusual," Mom said.

Agnes looked up from the photo, squinting for a few seconds as her eyes adjusted. "Oh yes, they are, aren't they? It's a new venture of mine. I repurpose old quill pens into newer fountain pens. Of course, I can make them into rollerball pens too, but those aren't nearly as much fun as a good old fountain pen."

"Nifty." Millie tapped her finger on the phone bringing Agnes' attention back to the buckle.

"Do you have an old pen you need repurposed? I'm having a sale. Lots of people are taking advantage of it," Agnes said. "I'm turning Anita Pendragon's great-great-great-grandfather's sterling silver quill pen into a fountain pen and Leslie Bruber's mother-in-law is have me retrofit her grandmother's old mother of pearl pen, too."

"No, thanks," Millie said.

"Oh and I repurpose old buckles and buttons into jewelry as well." Agnes beamed with pride. "I could show you some if you'd like."

"We'd love to," Millie said. "But not today. Today we'd like to know about *this* buckle. Perhaps you worked on it recently, restored it for someone, maybe?"

As Agnes stared down at the buckle again I looked at the pens. They appeared to be ancient. A few were made of horn, one looked like etched silver. My gaze fell on a purple card sticking out from the bottom of the display. It had a crystal ball on it with a Milky Way of stars swirling around it. I pulled it out further to see the name. Esther Hill! Had she been here for a buckle?

"That's an old buckle," Agnes said. "But this is a drawing, not a photograph, they didn't have them back then."

"Yes, we know." Millie sounded impatient. "But the drawing is so realistic, we figure the artist drew the buckle exactly."

"My guess is the buckle is from the early seventeen hundreds. You know they handmade them back then. Usually out of brass, then they would plate them with silver or gilt them with gold. This image is fuzzy and it's hard to see the fine details, but you can see the intricate work on the top," Agnes said.

"Yeah, we already figured all that. What we want to know is if anyone came in here and bought a buckle that looked like this," said Millie.

Agnes put her magnifying glass down. "Nope."

"You sound awfully certain. Don't you want to think about it, maybe check some records?" Millie said.

"Don't have to. I just thought about this the other day."

"You did?"

"Yep. Anita Pendragon was in here asking all about Jedediah Biddeford and his treasure. Luckily, I already had a lot of information out on him from a few weeks ago when the skeleton was found." Agnes pointed to a pile of papers and a book. "So, it's fresh in my brain and I would've remembered if someone bought buckles just like this."

"Anita was here asking about Jedediah?" Mom asked, her eyes widening as she nodded at Millie. Clearly this moved Anita up the suspect list.

Agnes pushed the phone toward Millie and bent down to store the magnifying glass back under the shelf. "Yeah, probably had something to do with that television producer."

"Television producer." This was the first I'd heard of that and the notion set my mind spinning.

Agnes nodded. "I don't remember his name. Some muckety-muck in a suit. He came in and wanted to know about Jedediah Biddeford, too. Asked all about the Oyster Cove Guesthouse. Wanted to know all about the skeleton. He even bought a pen for my trouble. Good thing too, it's important that these high falutin' types realize information isn't free."

"He asked about the guesthouse?" This did not bode well. A movie about murders at the guesthouse would hardly bring in more guests. Or would it? One thing it would do is generate a lot of money for someone... maybe for the psychic who could talk to Jed. Had Madame Zenda known about the movie? Clearly Anita had.

"Yep, sounded like he was fixing to make a movie or a TV show or something. Kept asking about all this ghost business that you have going on over there with those psychics."

The mention of the psychics reminded me that Esther had been here. She hadn't been looking for a buckle, unless Agnes was lying or her memory was off, but did she know about the movie producer? I slid her card out from under the pen display and held it up. "And Esther Hill, what was she doing here?"

Agnes frowned and snatched the card out of my hand. "That there is confidential information. I don't tell on my clients. You should know that, missy."

All-righty then.

Mom gave me an I-raised-you-better-than-that scowl.

"Right. I was just wondering if maybe she overheard the movie producer asking about Jed's ghost."

Agnes shoved the card under the table. "Hard telling. Lots of people were here when that producer fellow came in and later on he was over at Annie's clam shack making a big deal about how important he was. Half the town heard him then." She paused for a few beats. "Is there anything else I can help you with?"

"No. Thanks for the information." Millie turned and we followed her out.

Outside in the street, Mom turned to us. "Do you really think someone is considering making the story about the skeleton into a movie? That could be quite lucrative and might even be good for business."

Millie nodded. "And we all know that money is a prime motive for murder, but the question is… who knew about the movie?"

"Anita Pendragon did. Agnes said she was in the shop, she might have overheard and she was first on the scene with the body. She's a reporter too and would know how to cover things up and make it look like she only discovered the body when she's really the killer," Mom said.

Millie started walking toward the car. "That's probably why she was hanging around the guesthouse so she could be the first to scoop a story when one of them talked to Jed. Then she could partner with the movie producer and get her ten minutes of fame."

"Esther knew too," I said. "Or at least she could have known. Her card was at the antique store and Agnes was quite secretive about why it was there."

"I still say that Pendragon and Madame Zenda where in cahoots," Millie said. "That's why Zenda was yelling out the window about her meeting with Jed."

Mom nodded. "Probably knew about the movie and wanted to make sure Anita covered it so that word would get back to the producer."

"I just hope that sourpuss Myron Remington doesn't think the publicity would put people off from booking a room at the guesthouse," Millie said.

I cringed. "Unfortunately Myron might be right. I got a cancellation just this morning."

Millie stopped in her tracks. "You did? Did they say why? Maybe it had nothing to do with all the murders."

"They didn't say specifically but it sounded like they were making up an excuse."

Mom patted my arm. "Don't worry, dear. Once word gets out about a movie, people will be flocking to stay at the guesthouse. People like to see where a movie took place."

I hoped she was right, but something in my gut said otherwise. "We don't even know if there will be a movie and in the meantime I've had three murders this summer. No wonder people are getting nervous. We need to figure out who killed Madame Zenda ASAP so we can get this whole thing out of the headlines."

"Good point," Mom said. "People have short memories. Once this is all over then it won't take them long to forget. Unless of course the movie producer wants to use the guesthouse as a movie set."

What were the odds of that? Slim, I'd say. I was still hoping for a quick resolution and things to go back to pre-murder normal.

"I say the buckle is the key." Millie walked down the sidewalk at a snail's pace as we talked.

"Yeah, but no one was looking for a buckle," Mom said.

Millie stopped in front of the candy store and turned to face Mom and me. "Not that we've found *so far*." Millie's face took on a look of determination. "We'll just have to keep looking. Meanwhile, I think we'd better take a closer look at our suspects and figure out who had the strongest motive to kill Madame Zenda."

Chapter Twelve

"What do you think Josie is doing in the antique store?" Marlowe asked as they turned down a side alley that led to the docks and their ultimate destination of the bait wharf, where they would meet with the rest of the Oyster Cove cats. By now the cats would have heard about the murder and be working on the case. Nero figured Harry would bring Louie Two Paws, the Siamese cat that hung out at the police station. They were hoping to get a scoop on what the police knew about the investigation so far.

Nero glanced back over his shoulder. Catching Josie's eye, he gave her a slight nod. "Must be about the buckle."

"Looks like Josie's catching on to this investigating thing. Maybe she won't need our help after all," Marlowe said.

Nero glanced at Marlowe, thinking she couldn't possibly be serious, before the two cats let out a string of meows that indicated how hilarious the notion was. "Imagine that, the humans not needing our help!"

The cats turned down Ocean Avenue and then took another alley to the bait wharf. It was mid-morning, so most of the fishermen were out in their boats and the wharf was quiet, except for the slapping of waves against the side of the wooden docks and the cawing of gulls. Nero was trying to avoid the gulls. He glanced up to make sure one wasn't swooping down on him as the delicious smell of rotting fish drew the two cats closer to their favorite secluded spot behind the large tuna scale that hung from a tall post.

The rest of the cats were already there. Juliette, the gray cat with a white diamond on her forehead, sat atop a stack of lobster traps, her fluffy gray tail dangling over the edge. Below her, Poe with his bright green eyes was finishing off the tail of a fish—haddock it looked like to Nero. Boots sat on another lobster trap, watching them approach with his usual superior manner. Truth be told, Boots and Nero had a bit of a rivalry going on, as they were both black with white markings. Nero, however, had the white tuxedo on his chest and Boots only had white on his paws. Nero figured that Boots felt inferior because of this and that's why he acted so obnoxious.

Stubbs, the ginger cat, wiggled his stub of a tail and nodded at Nero and Marlowe. Beside him, Harry, the fluffy Maine Coon, picked a burr off his tail. Fluffy tails were nice for show, but they did tend to collect all kinds of burrs and twigs and could easily become painfully matted.

Louie Two Paws, a sleek seal-point Siamese, lounged in a patch of sun. His paws were splayed out in front of him and the extra toes made it look like he was wearing furry mittens. The velvety brown points of his ears matched the mask on his face, which highlighted his extraordinary sapphire blue eyes.

"Hey, Louie, how's it going?" Nero asked as he plopped down beside Stubbs.

"Going pretty good." Louie licked one of his paws. He was always doing that to call attention to their uniqueness. Apparently this impressed the female felines. "I was just telling the others that I got into the evidence room and sniffed the evidence. The murder weapon didn't have any unique identifying scents on it, but that buckle was interesting."

"How so?" Nero asked.

"That thing is old as the hills."

"So it's not a replica that someone picked up to make it seem like it was Jed's?" Marlowe asked.

Louie shook his head. "Nope. That thing has to be about three hundred years old. It smells like antique molasses and old regrets. No fingerprints on the murder weapon. The note, of course, was not blood. Drippy red ink."

"Of course," Nero said. He'd thought he'd smelled as much on the body, but couldn't be sure with the actual blood smell from the wound.

"And what information do *you* have?" Poe preened his long curly whiskers fastidiously as he addressed Nero. "Have you set your superior intellect into figuring out if the killer is one of the guests at the guesthouse?"

"Yeah, seems like one of those kooky guests would be the perp." Harry liked to use old detective slang. His human was an older gentleman and liked to read Dashiell Hammett and Raymond Chandler aloud to the cat. Apparently he'd picked up the lingo.

"Well, they sure are kooky." Nero couldn't argue with the other cat's assessment.

"And they did seem to be in competition to see who could talk to Jed's ghost. However, we have an inside scoop about that." Marlowe puffed up proudly.

Juliette raised a brow. "Do tell."

Marlowe's tail swished back and forth and her tone took on an air of importance. "We talked to Jedediah Biddeford's ghost himself. Turns out he hasn't spoken to any of them."

"Not even Madame Zenda?" Poe asked.

"Nope, she made it up."

"Humans always confound me," Harry said. "Why would anyone lie about talking to a ghost?"

Juliette hopped down from the lobster trap, her pads making a soft thud as she landed on the wharf. Her eyes gleamed with excitement as she causally said, "Maybe it has something to do with the movie."

"Movie?" Boots must have been surprised at that news because he lost his grip on the whiskers he'd been grooming and they sprung back into a tight curl. He quickly set about smoothing them again.

Juliette fluffed her tail. "Yes, a producer was in to talk with Father Tim about a movie he wants to produce about Jed's ghost and the treasure. He wanted to set some of the scenes in the church and cemetery."

"Why would they set scenes in the church?" Stubbs asked.

Juliette shrugged. "Who knows? At first, Father Tim didn't like the whole idea. He felt it was sacrilegious, but then the producer mentioned the donation to St. Michael's could be quite hefty. Apparently a movie like this would make a lot of money."

"Ahhh, money." Boots started pacing. "It's usually the root of the crime. That explains why all these psychics are really here. They must have gotten wind of the movie and wanted to reap the rewards. Madame Zenda lied so she could be the one in the spotlight."

"And someone else wanted to make sure she didn't get it, so they offed her," Stubbs said.

"But it might not be one of the guests," Nero pointed out. "Anita Pendragon has been lurking around the place too."

"And she was the first one to discover the body," Marlowe added.

"The director did say it could make any of the people involved very famous." Juliet trotted over to a lobster trap and poked around inside for any scraps of bait that might be left.

"People?" Marlowe's eyes narrowed. "What about cats? We're the ones that Jed is actually talking to!"

"Don't be silly, cats never get credit. But if they did have cats they would use feline actors just like they use human actors for people." Juliette fluffed up her tail to its fullest. Nero thought it looked like a long gray toilet brush, but Juliette claimed that her fluffy tail was a sign of delicate beauty. "They try to choose cats that have a certain aesthetic appeal. I was thinking I could play Nero if I get discovered. I tried to call attention to myself by jumping on the producer's lap and fluffing my tail in his face but all he did was sneeze and shoo me away."

Boots preened his whiskers. "Just as well. I think I would be a better choice. They need a cat with brains."

Nero scowled at Boots. *Was that a compliment or an insult?*

Boots continued, "Hopefully they'd pick actors that look better than the actual people, too. Take that Victor with his odd mustache. He won't look good on the big screen." Boots patted his mustache with his paw as if to highlight how much better looking his tache was.

"Your mustache is much nicer than that Victor's," Juliet said.

The other cats rolled their eyes, echoing Nero's thoughts that Juliette didn't need to inflate Boots' ego any more than it already was.

"You've seen Victor?" Harry asked. Good point. When had the other cats seen Victor?

"Yes. Father Tim and the producer were talking on the church steps and I was trying to highlight my acting abilities by skulking in the bushes when I startled a man who appeared to be lurking around the corner of the church. I thought he was eavesdropping, but then he came right over to Father Tim and introduced himself."

"Did he say why he was there?" Harry asked.

"Not really. He had on the most luxurious velvet jogging suit in a deep plum. I couldn't help but run my paws over it." Juliette sighed and looked off into the distance as if remembering the soft feel of the velvet. "I think he was hinting around at playing the lead in the movie though."

Nero's whiskers twitched. "Victor was at the church? Was this before or after Madame Zenda was murdered?"

"Oh, it was before. That very morning, in fact," Juliette said.

Nero glanced at Marlowe. Victor knew about the movie. Funny though, Nero hadn't heard Victor mention that to the others. Which made him wonder just how far Victor would go to make sure he got the lead.

Chapter Thirteen

On the walk to the car, my phone rang. I pulled it out of my pocket and saw my daughter's name on the display. "Oh, it's Emma. I'm going to take this."

My mom's eyes lit up and she yelled into the phone as I was answering, "Hi, honey! Hope you're having a good time."

"Was that Grandma?" Emma asked as I pressed the phone to my ear and sidled away from my mother.

"Yep, we're downtown shopping." I moved further away because my mother looked as if she was going to grab the phone. Mom was in the habit of blurting out all kinds of things to Emma that I really wished she wouldn't. Like things about dead bodies in the guesthouse and my non-existent love life.

"I talked to her earlier. I hear you have another dead body, another murder," Emma said.

See what I mean?

"Oh that? It's nothing to worry about. The police have it under control." I glanced back at Mom and Millie who were obviously listening in. The raised brow look they shared didn't escape me and I moved further away.

"Well, if you say so, Mom. I guess by now you know how to handle them." Emma laughed. "I just wanted to check in and make sure you were okay."

I couldn't help but smile. I was touched that my grown daughter, who now worked for the FBI, was checking in on me. "I'm fine!" I hoped my forced, chipper tone didn't come across as sounding false. "You know me, steady as she goes. Same old, same old."

"Uh-huh. So things are going good at the guesthouse? You're getting a lot of bookings?"

My stomach churned remembering the cancellation this morning. "Yes, it's going really well. The renovations are on track and pretty soon I'll have made back my investment and be sitting pretty." A slight lie depending on one's definitions of *pretty soon* and *sitting pretty*.

"That's great, Mom."

"How are things going with you?" I steered the conversation to her, which was much more interesting for me anyway.

"Work is going great! I'm getting a vacation in a couple of months and I thought I'd come out and visit."

Panic shot through me. What would happen when she came to visit? Would there be a dead body? Would she and my mother gang up on me about Mike? I took a deep breath. She'd said a couple of months. No need to panic now. Besides, my desire to see my daughter outweighed everything else. "That would be great."

"Okay. Good. We'll make plans later on. Gotta run, break time is over." She clicked off and I put the phone back in my pocket.

"Emma is doing good, it seems," Mom said.

"Yes, she is." I knew Mom wanted to know more about the conversation, but I wasn't going to give her that satisfaction. Besides, she'd already overheard everything on my end.

Millie had wandered down two stores and was gesturing toward the window. "Boodles is having a huge purse sale!"

Mom rushed over and I followed at a more sedate pace. The store was a cute boutique with a pink-and-yellow striped awning and displays of designer purses in the window. A little red leather clutch with a studded butterfly design caught my eye, but the last thing I could afford was to buy a purse—especially now that someone had cancelled.

"You guys go ahead and shop. I'm going to visit with Jen at the post office."

"Okay, dear, we'll meet you there in a half hour," Millie called over her shoulder, as she disappeared into the store.

Jen Summers had been my best friend all through school. Even when I'd moved away, we'd kept in touch. One of the positive things about moving back was reconnecting with her and it was as if the decades in between had never happened.

Jen was the postmistress for Oyster Cove, and I have to admit that did come in handy when investigating a murder, as I'd found myself doing all too often this summer. The post office was the grapevine for the town and if there was anything to be learned about this movie producer or the murder at the guesthouse, I'd hear it there.

As I opened the door to the old brick post office, Mrs. Pennyfeather was leaving. I held the door and she scooted as far away from me as she could, crossed herself and rushed out into the street.

Jen was behind the counter.

"What's with Mrs. Pennyfeather?"

Jen's left brow quirked up. "Words gotten out you had another murder and something about a ghost. I think she's a little worried you might be the devil."

"Great. Is that what people are saying?" I crossed the old black-and-white marble floors to the counter. The Oyster Cove post office was a wonderful throwback to the 1930s, with its oak-paneled doors, wainscoting, brass fixtures, gold stenciling and frosted glass. It even had the vanilla-tinged scent of old paper.

Jen was replacing the roll of labels in the machine that printed out priority mail stickers. "It's no secret that you have all those psychics and mediums up at your place. They've been running around town telling fortunes and offering to contact deceased relatives."

"Yeah. But no ghost."

"So you say. People seem to think there really is one, though. What happened?"

I told her all about my unusual guests and included the details of how we'd found Madame Zenda with the note and buckle.

"Agnes Withington just told us that a television producer is in town asking about the guesthouse. I think it's weird timing, especially with Anita Pendragon lurking around outside the mansion." I picked a chocolate kiss out of the bowl Jen kept on the counter. Today she had the ones with the almonds inside. I like the solid chocolate better, but beggars can't be choosers.

"What was she doing there?" Jen squinted into the machine and pulled out a ripped piece of sticker backing.

"At first I assumed she was trying to get information for a story. The psychic guests came because of the discovery of Jed's skeleton. They're attempting to communicate with him and find out where the treasure is." I popped another kiss into my mouth. "But seeing as she's the one that found Madame Zenda's body and claims not to have seen anyone else around…"

Jen glanced up at me from the machine. "You think she could've killed her? Why? Seems like she'd want to keep her alive so she could get the story from Jed."

Jen had a point. If Anita thought there really was a ghost and she killed off Madame Zenda, she'd be killing off the cash cow. "I think all this ghost business is malarkey. Someone is just hyping it up for their own purposes. What if Anita found out Madame Zenda was a fake? She saw all her hopes for an exclusive article and possibly selling the rights to the movie producer go out the window, so she killed her and staged it so she could make up some story about how the ghost killed Madame Zenda."

Jen pointed to the *Oyster Cove Gazette* on the counter. "She's already published the story. Front page, too."

I glanced over to see the headline: *Ghostly Murder at Oyster Cove Guesthouse.* That was sure to go over great with Myron and any potential guests.

Jen slammed the machine shut and pressed a button. The stickers advanced and she ripped off the first one and then leaned against the counter opposite me. "What are the police saying?"

"Millie hasn't been able to get anything out of Seth thus far."

"Maybe Millie needs to ramp up her efforts to extract information from him." Jen was quite familiar with the methods Millie used to get information out of Seth and we both made a face. Neither one of us needed that visualization.

"I just hope it gets solved quickly. Myron seems very nervous about the loan. He's afraid that it'll hurt business at the guesthouse and I won't be able to make the monthly payments."

"Myron's annoying. Maybe it will help business."

"I don't know. Someone did cancel this morning."

"Maybe they were sick or getting a divorce or had some other reason to cancel." Jen's gaze drifted over my shoulder and the lines around her lips tightened. "Crap. Here he comes now."

"Who?" I turned around just as Myron opened the door and trotted in, trailing an air of importance behind him.

"Josie! I'm glad I've caught you here," Myron said.

"Me too," I lied.

"I need to talk to you about this business at the guesthouse. I'm very worried."

"There's nothing to worry about, Myron. It's just a simple murder. I mean, it's highly unlikely word would get out to anyone coming here to stay. Most of the guests are from out of town." I leaned my arm on the paper to cover up the headline just in case he hadn't seen it yet and conveniently didn't mention the cancellation from that morning.

Myron scowled. "Be that as it may, it's no good having those people in the guesthouse. You don't know what they're going to do next. Maybe even something ungodly like a seance. I say you need to get rid of them before something else happens."

"What could possibly happen that's worse than a murder?" I asked.

Myron shuddered. "Who knows with that ghost running about and all that."

"Myron, you don't actually believe in ghosts, do you?" Jen asked.

Myron straightened his blue silk paisley tie and pursed his lips together. "Of course not, but something's going on up there and it's not good." He turned to me. "Anyway, I need to stop by later. I left my pen and notebook there and I need my notes."

"Okay, I'm heading back soon." The thought of seeing Myron twice in one day was not appealing; maybe I could just put his pen and notebook in the foyer.

The door opened and Mom and Millie bustled in, narrowing their eyes at Myron.

"Myron." Millie nodded at him, then turned to me. "Josie, it's time to go now. Are you ready?"

"Definitely." I waved at Jen and let them pull me away. When I got to the door, I looked over my shoulder at Myron. "Stop by anytime. I'm headed home now."

Outside Millie let go of my elbow. "He's stopping by? Told you he had a crush."

"Never mind Myron. Did you find anything out from Jen?" Mom asked.

"I didn't find out much. Except that the murder and the ghost made the headlines. And it appears that Myron is getting more nervous about the loan he gave me."

Chapter Fourteen

Nero usually didn't spend much time in the attic unless he was hunting for mice. The small dormer windows didn't let in enough sun for his liking and the smorgasbord of smells from the generations of people who had cast away their belongings was distracting.

The space was packed with broken old furniture, old clothing and various household items. Had no one who lived in this house ever thrown anything away? And the dust! It lay thick like a carpet on the floor, especially in the back area where the oldest items were. Nero had to tread carefully so as not to stir up too much of it. He didn't want to get dirt on his pristine, white tuxedo chest.

"Seems like you're getting kind of famous around town," Marlowe said as she detoured over to sniff a pile of books. On their way back to the guesthouse, the cats had heard the townspeople gossiping about Jed's ghost and the recent murder. Some were even talking about the treasure again, but no one seemed eager to look for it, thinking that Jed's ghost was out to kill anyone who did.

"Someone is even talking about making a movie," Nero added. Jed's swirling form jerked in dismay. "I don't think I want to be famous. I'm getting a bit tired of this old place now. I think I want to move on to whatever one moves on to."

"Well then, why are you still here?" Marlowe asked.

"Good question. I feel like I'm stuck here for some reason," Jed said.

"Unresolved issue," Nero said. "There was only one reason for ghosts to hang around and that was an unresolved issue. In Jed's case it made perfect sense because he'd been murdered. "Probably you want your killer named. You have no idea who it is?"

Jed shook his head. "None at all. I vaguely remember returning from Europe. I had that treasure, you know. But I didn't trust too many people, so I buried it before anyone knew I was back in town. I had to keep it all a secret because I knew people were watching me."

Marlowe's eyes grew large. "They were? Who?"

Jed glanced around uneasily as if those people were still around watching him. "People in my own household."

"You don't say," Nero said. They'd come to the very end of the attic where the light from the east filtered in through a perfectly formed spider web in the round window at the peak of the eaves. Here, the cast-offs were older and much more worn. Newspapers as brittle as dried leaves were piled in one corner. Wooden chairs hung from hooks on the wall, the wicker caning in the seats and backs broken and hanging down. An old steamer trunk sat in the corner practically disintegrating.

"Oh, it's true." Jed stood up straighter. "Course, I knew Helena—that's my wife—might've been up to something while I was gone. She was none too happy about my trip to Europe."

"Do you think she killed you?" Marlowe's tail swished, sending particles from a patch of dust on the floor into the air.

Jed pondered that for a few seconds and Nero wondered what kind of woman his wife had been. Had she been mad enough to kill? And what happened to her after Jed's death? Judging by the way the trunk had been shoved in the corner she might have packed up his things and forgotten about him. But that had nothing to do with the current happenings at the guesthouse... or did it?

"Don't rightly know." Jed glanced at the trunk. "I was shut up in that wall until now so I don't know what became of her. I don't think she had the skills to plaster a body inside a wall though."

"She might have had an accomplice," Marlowe suggested.

"If that's true, they probably took the treasure," Nero said. He was certain there was no buried treasure on the property as he would have sniffed it out by now. Treasure had a certain hopeful smell to it.

Jed swirled over to the trunk and sat on top of it. "Course that doesn't explain why someone took my best pair of shoes."

Nero thought about the buckle. "You mean the fancy ones with the buckle on them?"

"Yep."

"And they were in this trunk?" Nero inspected the latches. They were broken so someone could get in easily, the only problem was he didn't see or smell any recent sign of humans. If someone took Jed's shoes to plant the buckle on Madame Zenda, then wouldn't there be some sign? And how would they even know the shoes were in there?

Jed looked down at the trunk. "You can see all my good clothes are in there, but no shoes."

"Actually, we can't see." Marlowe gestured toward the trunk. "It's closed."

Jed stood and the three of them pushed on the top of the trunk. It was heavy and Nero was careful to keep his claws in lest he break a nail on the old wood. Beside him Jed grunted and struggled, beads of ectoplasmic sweat dripping from his brow. How had Jed gotten the trunk open all by himself before?

Finally, the hinges creaked and the trunk opened. Jed pointed to the deteriorating contents. "See? No shoes."

Nero and Marlowe hopped inside, carefully pawing through the musty old fabric. The clothing had been chewed by moths and was frayed at the edges, but Nero could see it had once been good quality. A suit, a silk robe and something that looked like a white linen slip. He slid his paw over it and glanced at Jed with his brow raised.

"What?" Jed's eyes flicked from Nero to the white linen. "That's my night shirt."

Nero wasted no time getting out of the trunk. It had been stifling inside there. After a fit of sneezing he looked up at Jed. "You're right. No shoes. I guess we should close it."

"Yep. Leave it the way it was," Jed agreed, but didn't make any effort to close the lid.

"Can you do it?" Nero asked, not because he was too lazy to help but because he wondered how Jed could have gotten it open and closed when he could barely push salt-and-pepper shakers off the table.

Jed pushed on the top of the trunk, but it only budged a few inches then fell back open. "Guess I need help."

Nero and Marlowe trotted over to the other side and between the three of them they pushed it closed with a loud thud that Nero was sure Josie could hear downstairs. "It took all three of us to close it," Nero said.

"Yeah. So?" Jed sat back down on the top of the trunk.

"If it took all three of us to open and all three of us to close it, then how did you know the shoes were missing?" Nero gave Jed one of his unblinking stares. "You wouldn't have been able to open the trunk."

Jed didn't even hesitate before answering. "Easy, I can just pass through to get inside."

"You can?" Marlowe batted at Jed's ankle, her paw passing right through the apparition. "Guess you aren't solid so that makes sense." Marlowe shrugged at Nero and then hopped up on top of a stack of old newspapers and proceeded to preen her tail.

"How do you think I get into rooms with closed doors? I can go pretty much anywhere it seems. Lucky thing too or I'd be stuck in that old ballroom and it's mighty boring in there," Jed said. He had a point. Jed had been going in and out of the west wing and the door to that wing was always closed. Plus he'd gotten into the locked attic with ease. Apparently he was telling the truth.

"Then how come you were stuck inside the wall all this time?" Nero asked. "If you can go through things, why not just come out?"

"I didn't know any better," Jed said. "I wish I had, but all I knew was I was in a dark place. Spent most of my time in limbo. It's kind of fun over there."

Nero supposed that could be true. Jed sure did look like he was telling the truth, but he cautioned himself. Ghosts were known to be sneaky.

"So, what did this buckle look like? Similar to the one found on Madame Zenda?" If no one had been here recently, had the shoes been taken long ago by Jed's wife? Was her ghost around trying to eke out some kind of revenge on Jed? Perhaps by killing Madame Zenda and trying to frame him by using the buckle. No. It was ludicrous. How could a ghost save a buckle for three hundred years?

Jed squinted, apparently thinking back to the buckle they'd found on the body. "Yep, near as I remember it was almost exact."

Marlowe stopped mid-preen. She'd had her leg lifted to get at the underside of her striped tail and was now staring down at the newspapers upon which she was perched. "Hey, are these the shoes here?"

Jed bent down, his face inches from the paper, to look at the paper. On the front page was an etching. It was the one Nero had seen in the town history book depicting the Oyster Cove Guesthouse back in Jed's day when it was a smaller family estate. Jed sat outside with his wife, children and some servants. It looked like he was wearing the outfit they'd seen in the trunk, though it was in much better shape.

"Yep, those are my good dress shoes. Only had one pair." Jed smiled. "I remember when that was drawn. The artist was quite good, captured everything perfectly. We had to sit still for a long time. Was hard on the children."

Nero summoned his cat-like powers of vision. The picture was grainy, but his super senses allowed him to see much clearer. "Yep, that's identical to the buckle we found on Madame Zenda."

"And Louie Two Paws said that buckle was three hundred years old," Marlowe said. "That means it could be Jed's actual buckle. I guess that's good. We know where the buckle came from."

Nero glanced back at the trunk. "But that doesn't bring us any closer to the most important questions. How did the killer get Jed's buckle and why did they put it on Madame Zenda's body?"

"True dat." Marlowe jumped down and padded off toward the stairs. "Only one way to find out. We need to get Josie up here so she can figure out the buckle came from Jed's trunk herself."

Chapter Fifteen

I filled in Mom and Millie on what I'd found out at the post office on our way back to the guesthouse.

"You'd think if they were real psychics they'd know who killed Madame Zenda," Millie said as we let ourselves in through the back door in the kitchen.

"Good point," Mom said. "Kinda proves they're fakes."

"Which means the killer wasn't a ghost," I added.

Thud!

We all looked up at the ceiling. "Did that come from the attic?" Mom asked.

"Don't think so. Kind of loud." Millie walked around the kitchen, her eyes still glued to the ceiling. "I'd be surprised if we could hear something from the attic two floors below."

"Must be the cats," Mom said.

Of course it was the cats, you never knew what they would be getting up to, though usually they were a lot more silent and sneaky.

"Probably knocked something over." Millie turned her attention away from the ceiling, opened the fridge and started to rummage around. "Have you thought about what you'll serve for breakfast tomorrow? Even with all this going on the guesthouse has to keep its reputation for fine breakfasts. We don't need to have another reason for people to think about canceling."

Shoot! I'd completely forgotten about that. My mind raced to think up the quickest and easiest meal, but I didn't want Millie to know I was thinking 'quick and easy'. "I was thinking we should go with something that I can heat up in the morning, like a frittata. And then I could make some waffles too. The sugar will set off those feel-good endorphins and they won't be worried about the fact that one of them could get murdered next."

Millie scowled at me. "Do you really think someone else might get murdered? It looked like Madame Zenda's murder had a specific purpose."

"Yeah," Mom chimed in. "I don't think anyone else is in danger."

"Probably not, but I can whip up the batter in the morning and cook them hot in the waffle maker for them. I have some spinach I need to use up, I can put that in the eggs." No sense in wasting food, and I needed to be frugal, just in case.

"Sounds good." Millie disappeared into the fridge and came out with the ingredients for the frittata.

Mom pushed in beside Millie and pulled out some string cheese. "That's smart thinking," she said as she pulled off a string from the cheese and dangled it into her mouth. "Everyone loves a sweet and savory combo and maybe that will have them raving about the breakfast and talking about the dead body not so much."

Millie put the spinach, eggs, milk and cheese on the counter and preheated the oven.

The cats appeared in the kitchen and trotted over to sniff at the oven, then fixed me with their intelligent eyes. I was relieved to see that Nero had dust on his whiskers, indicating that it had probably been them that caused the thud. It looked like they *had* been in the attic. I knew it was dusty in there. Not that I was worried about it being a ghost or anything, more like a nosey guest. Or Anita Pendragon. How the cats had gotten in there, I had no idea. Maybe there was a secret passage or something. Come to think of it, one of those old servants' rooms had a door with a crack in it that led straight to the attic, the cats could probably fit through that.

Millie bent down to pet them, but they had another agenda.

Meow. Nero glanced at me, then trotted over to the narrow servants' stairs that led to the attic.

Meroop. Marlowe was right behind him, her tail fluffed up as she trotted ahead of Nero, then looked back as if to see if we were following.

Nero kept giving me the eye. I thought back to the previous murders. Each time someone had been murdered the cats had seemed to be suggesting things to me. I could have sworn they'd helped me out of a few scrapes, maybe even saved my life. I was starting to believe that what Millie had said about cats being smarter than humans was true. Maybe I should take their advice under consideration. And right now, it looked as if they wanted me to follow them upstairs.

I was just starting toward the stairs when Myron's voice bellowed from the foyer. "Josie! I'm here for my notebook."

Millie's face scrunched up. "Is that Myron Remington?"

"Yeah, he mentioned he had left his notebook and pen here." I reluctantly turned away from the stairs, ignoring the protesting meows and exasperated looks from the cats.

"Can't he get a new notebook?" Mom asked. "Such a cheapskate."

"Well he does like the finer things. Did you see his notebook has a leather cover and that pen looks very old and expensive." Millie focused on beating the eggs and I left the two of them in the kitchen and headed to the foyer to meet Myron.

"I see a murder hasn't scared these people off yet," Myron said when he saw me coming down the hall. Unfortunately, he said it loud enough for the people in the parlor to hear him.

Victor called out from his spot next to the fireplace where he was sitting in a chair swinging some sort of talisman in the air. "Scare us off? No way. Now more than ever I know that I'll be able to communicate with Jed and solve the mystery not only of his death and where the treasure is buried, but also who killed Madame Zenda or Betty Sue or whatever her name was."

"What do you mean?" Gail asked. "I thought Jed killed Madame Zenda."

Victor waved his hand in the air. "I doubt it, but if he did I suppose he will confess to me."

Esther had been sitting over by the table with her crystal ball in front of her. The cats must've followed me into the hallway because they were now both sitting in her lap. She was petting and cooing to them.

She eyed her crystal ball and softly said, "Don't think that you're the only one who can talk to Jed. You might be surprised at who else has psychic abilities."

Victor jerked his head in her direction. "I'm not worried about you wannabes. I know I'm the only real psychic and so does everyone else."

He glanced out the window and I followed his gaze and saw a swirl of pink. Anita Pendragon? I'd have thought the murder would have scared her off. Especially if she was the killer. But apparently the chance of getting a story scoop that could be made into a movie was too enticing.

I also noticed the window was open again, even though Flora and I had been making sure we kept them closed. Did Anita have a cohort inside that left it open so that she could overhear our conversations? For all I knew she was taping everything we said.

"So no one is leaving then?" Myron asked.

They all shook their heads.

Myron glanced at me and I smiled. This was good. Now that Myron knew that the guests weren't scared off, maybe he'd curtail any thoughts about canceling the loan. I didn't need to mention the cancellation I'd already gotten. That was probably a fluke.

"The only thing that would get us to leave is if the real ghost was here trying to kill off another one of us." Gail frowned down into her mug, apparently reading something she didn't like in the tea leaves.

Millie had come down the hall and was standing next to me. Mom was right behind her. "Good thing that so far he doesn't seem interested in killing anyone."

Thunk!

Another candlestick fell off the mantle and we all looked at it suspiciously. Even the cats seemed distrustful of the fallen object.

Gail picked it up and put it back. "Weird."

I could practically see thoughts of hauntings whirling in Myron's head. Luckily there had been no other signs of a ghost— like eerie moans or lights flickering. At least I had that on my side.

Victor stared at the candlestick. "Say, is anything in here an item that belonged to Jed? I can speak to the departed more easily if I am holding one of their objects, you know. Preferably something he favored."

I looked around the room. Most of the belongings had come with the sale. I glanced at Millie.

"Not anything in here. These things belonged to my family," she said.

Victor looked disappointed. Myron was staring at him with a mixture of dread and suspicion.

"So, Myron. You're probably in a hurry, I know how busy you are. I'll walk with you to the west wing to get your notebook and pen. You can see how nicely Ed is progressing with the work." I quickly ushered him down the hall. The less time Myron spent in the guesthouse the better as you never knew when the next weird thing was going to happen.

Myron's notepad and pen were right where he'd left them in the ballroom. Ed didn't appear to be keen on seeing Myron again, muttering something about Myron leaving them on purpose so he could have an excuse to come back and see me. I hoped he wasn't going to start leaving things around just so he could stop by. He'd been here enough in the past week already.

I tried to ignore Ed's mutterings as I shoved the pen and notepad into Myron's hand and then rushed him out the front door before anyone could say anything that might make him even more nervous about the financial situation at the guesthouse. I wanted him to leave on a high note thinking things weren't so bad. If the current guests weren't considering defecting from the guesthouse and staying at the Smugglers Cove Inn down the road, then it wouldn't harm future guests and therefore my loan.

When I returned to the kitchen Millie and Mom were getting ready to leave.

"We gotta run, Josie. It's bingo night tonight. I think you can handle the clean-up." Mom gestured to the countertop now littered with food scraps, dirty bowls and utensils. "The frittata is in the oven, don't forget to cover it when you reheat it tomorrow otherwise it will be too dry."

"Yep, no problem." I wondered if I could get Flora to do the dishes. Probably not. I'd heard her vacuuming upstairs earlier and I was sure she'd claim to be exhausted.

I set to work cleaning up, periodically checking the dish in the oven. I'd had a little bit of a problem with burning baked goods a few weeks ago and was extra cautious with cooking time as a result.

The clean-up gave me time to think. If these incidents were not due to a ghost—and I was sure they weren't because there was no such thing as ghosts—then *someone* had killed Madame Zenda. Would that person stop at one person? Was Madame Zenda killed because the person believed she could talk to Jed and wanted to stop her? Or was there some other reason that the murderer wanted her dead?

Maybe Madame Zenda knew something about one of them that the other person wanted to keep secret. Esther knew her real name, did someone else have a relationship with Madame Zenda that I didn't know about? I made a mental note to dig around on the Internet and see if I could find such a connection.

I knew one thing, the murder wasn't random. The note and the buckle proved that the killer had a specific reason to want her dead. Hopefully the killer would have no reason to strike again. Still, I was glad I had a double lock on my owner's quarters.

I was bent down peering into the oven for the umpteenth time when I heard the back door open. I whirled around, heart pounding. Apparently this murder business had me more nervous than I thought.

"Whoa, Sunshine. Didn't mean to startle you." Mike sauntered in, the lazy smile on his handsome face holding a hint of amusement at the way I'd jumped. My heart started beating even faster, but not because I thought he was the killer.

"You startled me." Nothing like stating the obvious.

His face immediately took on a look of concern. "Are you worried because of the murder? Do you not feel safe here? I could come and stay here if you want—"

I raised my palms in front of me and cut him off. "No. I'm not worried. I just wasn't expecting anyone to sneak up on me." I pulled the frittata out of the oven and set it on the counter.

"I wasn't sneaking up." His eyes narrowed. "Wait a minute... are you not worried because someone else is staying here?"

Now it was my turn to narrow my eyes. "What do you mean? There's a lot of people staying here. It's a guesthouse."

"Not them. I saw Myron leaving when I came in. He's been here a lot lately."

I made a face. Did Mike think I had something going on with Myron? Was he jealous? For some reason that amused me. I waved my hand dismissively as if Myron's presence was of no consequence. Which it was. "Oh yeah. He left his notepad and pen here and came to pick it up."

"Ummm... hmmm... I bet he did." Mike said it with the same hint of sarcasm in his voice that Ed had done when I brought Myron into the ballroom to retrieve his items.

"Did you want something?" I asked as Mike sauntered over to the counter and started picking at one of the leftover lemon muffins. I slapped his wrist. "Those are for guests."

"Mmmm... this is good. Your cooking has really improved."

I took a minute to bask in his compliment. "Thanks."

"I have some new information on the case."

I composed my face into a blank look and stared at him. I didn't fool him though because he said, "Forget playing dumb, Sunshine. I know that you, your mom and Aunt Millie are investigating."

I simply raised my brows. Mike had been an investigator in the navy and had gotten all bossy and protective when we'd tried to investigate the last two murders. Maybe he was getting used to the idea that when someone was killed on my property I looked into it. Good. Any help we could get would be welcome and

Mike knew how to investigate, plus his office was in the town hall and he could have access to insider information.

"So, what did you find out?" I asked after trying to wait him out.

"Turns out that buckle really was old," Mike said.

I frowned. "You mean like as old as Jed?" I glanced over at the stairs to the attic, remembering how the cats had been trying to lure me up there.

"Yep. Of course, it's probably not his, they have old buckles in antique stores and you can buy them on the Internet from eBay."

Of course! Why hadn't I thought of that? But if the killer got the buckle from eBay, then they would have had to purchase it way before the murder, as they would have had to have it shipped. Which meant that the murder might not have been because Madame Zenda said she was going to talk to Jed. It would have been planned before that.

Esther bubbled up to the top of my mental suspect list, but I cautioned myself not to jump the gun. Just because Esther had a prior connection to Madame Zenda didn't mean that she had a reason to kill her. Nor did it mean that the others didn't have prior connections. Hadn't Victor mentioned something about how her readings were never accurate? That seemed to indicate he was familiar with her work. And what about Gail? She'd been very quiet about her past and when I'd asked her once, she'd brushed me off. Besides, if Esther had murdered Madame Zenda because of some prior connection, wouldn't she have tried to hide the fact that she knew her?

"So the murder could have been planned for some time. If someone had researched Jed and his treasure and planned it out, maybe they had time to find a similar buckle."

Something outside the window caught my eye. Nero and Marlowe were slinking along the side of one of the old barns.

Stalking mice? Or something else? Up ahead of them, I saw a flutter of purple fabric. Anita Pendragon? No. It was Esther Hill. She was dodging from shrubbery to shrubbery. What was *she* up to?

"Josie?" Mike's question tugged my attention from the window.

"Huh?"

"I just said I think you should try to be careful here."

"Of course. I'm always careful."

Mike popped the last of the muffin into his mouth and brushed his hands together. "Okay, then. I guess I'll go see Ed."

"Ed?"

"Yeah, I came to inspect the ballroom. He's ready to start the electrics and I need to make sure the framing is right." His left brow quirked up. "Why did you think I was here?"

"Oh, I knew that was why, of course." With all the excitement, I'd forgotten about the planned inspection. I didn't want to explore the fact that I hadn't thought it odd that Mike had come, that it almost felt normal for him to just walk into the kitchen. With his connection to Millie and the guesthouse, it was natural he'd feel right at home.

He left and I returned my attention to the window. I couldn't see Esther or the cats anymore, but I couldn't help but wonder just what the three of them were up to out there.

Chapter Sixteen

Nero stared down into the empty hole in the ground. "Guess someone did take the treasure just like you thought."

Jed swirled beside him, his ghostly form tinged red with anger.

"Do you think it was one of the psychics?" Marlowe moved closer and sniffed, then shook her head. "No, can't be. The treasure scent in here is old, but the disappointment scent is new."

Nero agreed. As he had suspected all along, the treasure was long gone. They'd seen Esther dig the hole, so they knew she hadn't taken anything out, but even before that the ground had been packed down, the grass grown solid over the top. No one had dug here in many decades.

"Are you sure you told her the right location?" Nero glanced up at Jed cautiously. Jed had claimed that he'd successfully communicated with Esther through her crystal ball. He must have been telling the truth because Esther had come here and dug.

Jed scowled down at him. "Of course I know the right place. Sure, it took me a while to figure it out because the layout of the property has changed, but once I found the old outhouse, I paced it off and this is the spot. The big oak tree is gone, but you can see where it stood." Jed pointed to a round sunken depression in the ground. "This here is thirty paces northeast."

Nero and Marlowe nodded. Though the treasure was long gone, it could have been worse. Someone could have bought this old property and put up a strip mall and the hiding spot would be located under a parking lot. At least now they knew for sure that the treasure was gone.

Jed plopped down on the ground. Nero felt sorry for the ghost, he looked deflated. "Darn. I was hoping that pretty little Esther would dig the big treasure up."

"So you really did talk to Esther?" Nero said.

Jed nodded. "But she's the only one. I didn't talk to that loudmouth Victor. I wouldn't give him the time of day."

"Huh, then I wonder why he said you were talking to him," Marlowe said.

"Clearly it was for the television producer," Nero said. "That newspaper reporter has been hanging around outside and you know she's going to report back to him. Like Juliette said, Victor is setting himself up to be the star of the TV show." Nero was sure of it.

"Which makes me wonder how badly he wants that," Marlowe said.

Nero nodded. "Bad enough to kill."

"Exactly." Marlowe started pushing the dirt back into the hole with her paws and Nero joined her. They didn't want anyone to know that someone had been digging. Especially not that nosey Myron Remington who they'd seen traipsing all over the property. Nero didn't trust him one bit.

"Never mind that, we need to find out who killed *me*," Jed said. "I'm getting tired of hanging around here and something tells me I'm tied to this property until I figure that out."

"How do you expect us to figure out who killed you?" Marlowe said. "That was three hundred years ago."

"I don't know, but clearly someone killed me and took the treasure and given that some of my stuff is missing from the attic, I feel like the answer must be up there."

"I think that points to someone in your family." Nero thought about Jed's earlier accusation that his wife hadn't been happy with him. Had she killed him? How could they prove that?

Nero didn't mind putting some effort into that investigation, but his first priority was figuring out who had killed Madame Zenda. Could the two murders be related? Impossible, one had happened three hundred years ago... unless Jed's wife was really steamed at him and had waited three hundred years to get an even bigger revenge.

Nero closed his eyes and focused. He sniffed the air and waited for that twinge of the whiskers that told him something other-worldly was present. Nothing extra came through, just the vibrations from Jed.

"What on earth are you doing?" Marlowe asked. "We need to get Josie up into the attic so she can help us with the case. We can only do so much as cats. I know she was about to follow us up before Myron interrupted her."

The shadows were getting longer and Nero glanced to the west where the sun was just dipping below the horizon.

"Good thinking. But not tonight. It's almost dark and the attic is no place to be without the light of day to illuminate things." Nero didn't think Josie would like all those creepy shadows and dark corners. "I think our time is better spent searching the guests' rooms before they come back from dinner. First thing tomorrow, we will get Josie to the attic."

🐾

My favorite time of day was suppertime, mostly because I didn't have to serve it. The guests usually went out to eat and the giant mansion was quiet. Today was no exception and I was doubly glad because it gave me a chance to investigate the guests' prior connections to Madame Zenda.

For once, the cats weren't getting in the way. Usually they lay on my keyboard or stuck their tails in my face when I tried to use the computer, but tonight they were nowhere to be found. I wasn't sure what they were up to, but I could hear soft noises on the floors above as I sat in the back parlor, feet up on the coffee table and my laptop on my lap.

Up in the attic, perhaps? I remembered how they'd seemed to want me to follow them up there earlier in the day, and I had a vague notion that I should check the place out, but it was getting dark and I didn't know what the lighting situation was up there, so now wasn't a great time. Besides, something told me that I had to wait for the cats. If they had something to show me then they needed to lead the way.

Information on the guests was surprisingly easy to obtain, simply by googling. I guess when you are in a profession that depends on clients you have all your info out there. It wasn't much different for the Oyster Cove Guesthouse; I needed an Internet presence so people could find me. Apparently psychics needed that too.

As I'd already known, Madame Zenda and Esther had worked together a few times. Not that that should make me suspicious because Esther wasn't trying to hide the fact. She'd mentioned it right off. Except it hadn't been *right* off. It had only been after the murder. Initially the two of them had acted as if they barely knew each other and had exhibited the same undercurrent of animosity that I'd felt between all of the guests. Had Esther realized that the police would find the connection and made sure to mention it right away so as not to appear as if she was hiding something?

From what I could find on the Internet, they'd been crossing paths for over twenty years. Appearing on telethons together, local television shows and even a circus stint. I didn't find any bad press about either one of them.

Victor, on the other hand, had a more checkered past. I found the article from the *Dayton Ohio Examiner* about the scam that had been referred to earlier. Apparently, he'd been a personal psychic to a rich widow, Mary Chambers. He'd told her he was communicating with her dead husband. The widow's family had claimed he was a fraud and made a lot of commotion in the papers. There was talk of a lawsuit since Mary had paid him thousands. Mary passed away of natural causes and a lawsuit was never filed and nothing had ever happened to him, except a bunch of bad press.

According to the article, Victor had met the widow on a Dreams Divinity seven-day cruise. I'd never heard of them but apparently there were cruises that featured psychics. They gave group readings and passengers could hire them for private readings as well. Sounded like a perfect place to find a mark that would willingly spend money thinking you were letting them talk to their dead loved one.

A quick glance at some press for that particular cruise told me that Madame Zenda, Esther Hill and Victor Merino were listed among the featured mediums. Not Gail though. Interesting. Was it possible that Madame Zenda knew something about Victor's scam with the woman and Victor didn't want her to tell anyone? But why spill the beans now, when it was all in the past? A picture of some of the mediums and passengers on the cruise showed Victor smiling like the cat that ate the canary, his mustache even larger than it was now. Was he smiling because his plan to scam rich widows was well under way?

I googled Gail Weathers but couldn't find a thing. Odd… then again, Victor had eluded to her being an unknown. Maybe she was just starting out? She certainly did drink a lot of tea, so maybe she needed the practice.

Thud.

I jumped as a Murano glass paperweight rolled across the green-and-gold oriental rug. Must have toppled off of the side table. Instinctively I looked for the cats, but they weren't here. A cold chill crept up my spine, then I laughed. All this ghost talk was getting to me. Clearly the paperweight had just rolled off. Flora must have put it on its rounded side instead of on the flat bottom when she'd dusted.

I shut the laptop and headed to the kitchen to check that everything was in order for breakfast. I whipped up some waffle batter and put it in the fridge. I wanted to get the breakfast set up quickly the next morning so I could be ready to test out my suspicions that the cats really were trying to show me something in the attic.

"There's nothing in here but tea." Marlowe backed out from under the bed and sneezed. Nero glanced around the room. The other cat wasn't kidding; the place was loaded with tea tins. White, black, green, herbal. You name it and Gail had it in her room. It made him wonder why Gail was often seen in the kitchen pantry taking Josie's Earl Grey. Maybe she was just cheap.

"Well, that about does it. We've scoured all of the guests' rooms and haven't found one thing." Nero was disappointed. It wasn't as if he'd expected to find a smoking gun or anything, but if the killer was one of the guests wouldn't they have had paper that matched the note or a big red pen? Though a crafty killer would have thrown those things out...

Marlowe turned up her nose. "Other than that noxious cologne in Victor's room."

"That did smell horrid, but his velour lounging suits are soft to the touch." The velour was so soft, it must have been very high quality—clearly Victor Merino was a human that liked the finer things. Everything in his room had been top-notch, from the offending cologne to the expensive luggage to the clothing.

"So, what now?" Marlowe sat and looked at Nero with her head tilted to the side quizzically.

Nero glanced out the window. The moon had risen and cast a soft glow over the landscape. The guests weren't back yet, but he'd heard Josie knocking something over in the back parlor earlier and she was now rattling around in the kitchen. The guests would return any minute and it would only be a few hours before Josie went to bed, which meant they had a little time to go down to the bait wharf and meet with the other cats to find out if any of them had discovered anything.

"We meet the others." Nero headed toward the cat door that Millie had installed for them in the old storeroom on the first floor.

Nighttime was Nero's favorite time to visit the bait wharf. He loved the play of the moonlight on the waves and the fact that the gulls were all tucked in their nests—or wherever they went at night—and wouldn't be rudely swooping down on them.

When they arrived on the docks, Harry was sticking his paw in the water trying to skewer a fish with his sharpened claws. He did this all the time, although Nero didn't know why. It had only worked once and even then Harry had been so surprised that he fumbled the fish and it slipped back into the water with nary a backwards glance.

The gang was all there. Juliette lounged on the concrete slab under the tuna scale. It was probably still warm from the sun beating on it all day. Stubbs was curled up on top of a lobster trap, his tail around his nose. One green eye slid open as Nero and Marlowe approached. Poe and Boots had been batting around a piece of rope and they stopped and turned to Nero.

"Anymore news about that movie producer?" Nero asked.

Stubbs yawned and sat up. "I put a tail on that nosey dame reporter, Anita Pendragon. She met with that movie mogul. She's involved in something."

Nero nodded. No surprise there. "Has anyone picked up any other clues about the murder?"

Boots bestowed his look of superiority on them. "I have heard that it is someone closely tied to the guesthouse."

Marlowe practically rolled her eyes. "No one else in town knew her, so that's kind of a given."

Boots looked down his nose at Marlowe. "Are you sure about that?"

Marlowe frowned and glanced at Nero who nodded his head slightly. It was most likely that the killer knew Madame Zenda and he was certain she didn't know anyone in town.

"What about the buckle?" Nero asked.

"Nothing new on that," Harry said. "I talked to Louie Two Paws earlier today. The police haven't made much progress. They are checking out all those guests at the guesthouse. Seems that some of them have a shady past. But nothing new on the buckle."

Shady past. Nero wasn't surprised at that either. Judging by the way they acted so secretive amongst each other at the guesthouse, he knew they were the type that would often be up to something.

"What about you?" Juliette purred. "You're in the guesthouse with all of the suspects. Surely you have found out something by now? And have you followed up on my clue about your velvety jogging-suit wearing guest and the movie producer?"

"We didn't find anything in his room, but we do have something on the buckle that might be of interest," Marlowe said.

Poe turned to look at her. "Do tell."

"Jed's ghost verified that his shoes are missing from a trunk in the attic. The shoes with the buckle," Marlowe said. "Jed's suit is in there and all his other things, but no shoes."

"So someone has been in the attic," Stubbs said.

"Looks that way," Nero said. "Though I don't see how. Josie keeps it locked."

"And the buckle on Madame Zenda really was Jed's buckle?" Poe asked.

"Most likely," Nero said.

"Points to one of those guests even more," Juliette said. "But you found no indication in their rooms that they were the culprit? No drippy red pens or smells of old buckles?"

"No," Nero admitted. "But we have made another enlightening discovery."

The other cats stilled and looked at him in anticipation. He drew the moment out for a few seconds basking in the attention, then continued. "We know for sure that the treasure is long gone."

Boots frowned. "The ghost told you that?"

"Sort of. He suspected such and once he remembered exactly where he had buried it, he had one of the guests dig it up. Marlowe and I inspected the hole ourselves and it's been empty for centuries." Nero felt a bit sad about that. Josie could have used the money to complete renovations on the guesthouse. If she had treasure, she could get out from under Myron's thumb.

Juliette looked at him curiously. "So Jed *is* talking to the guests. They're not all frauds?"

"Nope. Turns out at least one, Esther Hill, really can talk to ghosts. Jed has been communicating with her through her crystal ball," Marlowe said.

"Is that so?" Boots tugged on his long whisker, curling it up at the ends in that showy way he preferred. "Well then, surely this Esther Hill has made it known that she can communicate with Jed? After all, that seems to be the reason they are all at the guesthouse, so they can earn their way to fame in the movie."

Nero and Marlowe exchanged a glance. Esther had been very quiet about her communications with Jed. She hadn't bragged once about talking to the ghost. "No, actually I don't think she has."

"Well, maybe not to anyone at the guesthouse," Marlowe said. "We don't know if she has mentioned it to Anita Pendragon. She might not want the others to know that she can talk to Jed because... well... look what happened to Madame Zenda after she announced that she was going to talk to him."

Nero nodded enthusiastically. He could have kicked himself for not thinking of that but was proud that Marlowe had. "Yeah. Good point."

Stubbs poked around in one of the lobster traps. "If Esther is keeping quiet because she's afraid the killer will target her next, then that means *she* isn't the killer."

"There's something else that may be in play here." Poe paced the outskirts of the group, his tail swishing, head down, apparently deep in thought.

"What?" they all asked.

He stopped and faced them. "Thus far, we've been assuming that Madame Zenda was killed because she said she could talk to Jed's ghost. Whoever killed her didn't want her talking to the ghost because they wanted the fame. A movie deal would be quite lucrative. Or that someone had a vendetta against her."

"We did determine that most of them have crossed paths before," Nero said.

"Yeah, Esther knew her real name," Marlowe added.

"And a movie deal could make them a lot of money." Juliette preened behind her ears. "Don't forget I did find the clue about Victor talking to the movie producer."

"How could we forget?" Poe asked. "But let us consider another reason. What if the murder wasn't about Madame Zenda at all? What if it was about the guesthouse?"

Nero didn't like the way that sounded. "What do you mean?"

"The body was found with the buckle and a warning to stay away from the guesthouse. Maybe that's what the killer really wanted—for people to stay away—and Madame Zenda just happened to be a convenient target."

"Why would someone want to scare people away from the guesthouse?" Marlowe asked.

Poe shrugged. "Beats me. But if I'm right, then whoever it is has a reason worth killing for."

Chapter Seventeen

The next morning breakfast went off without a hitch. The waffles came out golden brown and the guests slathered them in maple syrup and piled them on their plates. The frittata was cooked to perfection and not dry. *I might be getting the hang of this cooking business after all...*

I had a little bit of a scare when the cats started meowing in that way they do when something is wrong—like, for example, there's a dead body on the property—but thankfully everyone was accounted for and near as I could tell no bodies littered the grounds.

I hadn't forgotten about how the cats had tried to lure me to the attic, but they'd scattered after breakfast, so I decided to clean up while I waited for them to come back. I felt very strongly that wandering around up there by myself would be a waste of time. If the cats really did have something to show me, they'd be back.

Mom and Millie turned up while I was loading the last of the dishes into the dishwasher. It was a mystery to me as to how they usually ended up walking through the door just as I put the last dish in. They did have impeccable timing. I was too eager to tell them about my research from the night before and how I'd seen Esther sneaking around the property to marvel at how they always managed to get out of cleaning up. Maybe Flora had learned it from them.

"At least we know that Victor and Madame Zenda knew each other, but I suppose that's no big surprise. Why do you think Esther would be sneaking around?" Millie whispered after I told them about the cruise that Madame Zenda, Esther and Victor were on and how I'd seen Esther outside. "Maybe she was just out for a walk."

"Nope. She was definitely sneaking. Skulking along the shrubs and looking behind her," I said. "Looking for the trea—"

"Shhh!" Mom's eyes were wide and she was gesturing not so subtly over my shoulder. I turned to see Esther in the doorway.

"Well, I'm just irate!" Esther hadn't seemed to notice we'd been huddled in a group whispering.

"You are? Why?" I imagined all sorts of reasons she could be mad, ranging from the breakfast making her sick to Flora not cleaning her room properly to stumbling over another dead body. I prayed it wasn't the latter.

"That banker guy... Marvin somebody—" Esther said.

"Myron Remington," Mom said.

"Yeah, whoever. Short guy, owns the bank? I heard downtown at the post office that he's been badgering you." Esther turned kind eyes on me. She really did seem concerned about me and mad at Myron. Who could blame her? He did have a way about him that made people angry.

Millie didn't see Esther in the same light as I did, if her narrowed eyes and accusatory tone were any indication. "Just what were you doing at the post office?"

Esther blinked. "Mailing postcards. I always do that when I visit a new town."

"Oh." Millie looked disappointed that her question hadn't tripped up Esther, but I could see that she was assessing her to determine if she was lying about the postcards.

"Anyway, this place is so lovely I hate to think that nasty little man is being so controlling with the money. This magnificent house deserves to be restored." She lowered her voice. "I heard he was making noises about taking back your loan."

My heart twisted. Had that rumor been going around town? Esther could have easily heard it at the post office since that's where most rumors were spread.

"Well, I hope he isn't serious about that," I managed to squeak out.

"Me too. This place has great spirit vibes. Intelligent ghosts. Wonderful history." Esther's eyes sparkled.

Millie perked up. She always did when someone complimented the guesthouse. "It is a special place. And not just the inside, either. The grounds are lovely." Millie glanced out the window at the overgrown garden. "Well, the yard needs some work. Have you been out in the grounds at all?"

Esther looked down at her shoes. "Not really. I mean, I was out at Betty Sue's body and I've sat on the porch."

Maybe Millie was right to be suspicious because that was one whopper of a lie.

"What about the old buildings on the property? Some of them have great history." I gave her a chance to fess up. Maybe she just hadn't mentioned it or had forgotten.

"Oh no, I wouldn't go near any of those old buildings. Nope. Never ventured far from the house. Well, except when we found Betty Sue, of course." Esther cocked her head to the side as if listening to something in the hall. She seemed nervous. "I think I hear Victor. I better get back there. Wouldn't want him to get a leg up on talking to Jed's ghost. Good luck with your renovations."

Millie's brows shot up as Esther hurried out of the room. "Well, if that don't beat all. I say that woman has something to hide."

"She did seem genuinely concerned about the guesthouse." I really did think she was sincere about that.

"Probably a ploy to throw us off track," Mom said.

Meow!

Nero and Marlowe were sitting at the bottom of the back stairs; their unblinking gaze reminded me that I still hadn't had a chance to get up into the attic.

Millie rushed over to pet them, but apparently they had other things on their minds. They accepted a few quick pets on the head but then started to meow and pace around, putting one foot on the stairs and then glancing at us.

"I think they want to show us something," I said.

Mom looked at me funny, but Millie didn't seem the least bit fazed. "It's about time you started to understand their subtle communications. Hmmm... now let me see. It's the attic, right?" She addressed her question to Nero, who meowed loudly and started up the stairs.

We followed the cats up the narrow creaky stairs. No wonder I never took these things; the ceiling was low, the walls closed in. It was claustrophobic. I got a little winded by the second floor but Mom and Millie practically ran up and I didn't want to seem like a wimp, so I pressed on, even though the increase in temperature as we ascended caused sweat to drip down my back.

When we got to the top of the stairs I unlocked the door with the old skeleton key that I'd grabbed from the butler's pantry, and the door opened with an ominous creak.

I'd only been up in the attic once, when I had looked over the place to buy it, and then I'd only peeked in. Even though I'd spent a lot of time at the guesthouse as a little girl, the attic had held no interest for me and now I could see why. It was dusty and full of cobwebs. Big cobwebs. I looked around for the spiders that lived in them, but they must have all scurried to dark corners.

There must have been a dozen generations' cast-offs up here. During the negotiations to purchase the place, Millie had vaguely mentioned it came with all sorts of antiques and things I could use for the guesthouse. She'd made it sound like a bonus, but

I'd been skeptical. Turns out I was right, the place was crammed full of things that needed some sort of repair and a good clean.

Nero and Marlowe led us on a path between old pieces of furniture, lamps and boxes. They trotted straight to the oldest part of the house. I sneezed a dozen times as our footsteps kicked up dust from the thick layer that was on the floor. It was so thick that the cats' paws had made little prints in it as they'd walked ahead. I could see they'd been here a couple of times judging by the number of paw prints.

Up ahead, the cats were perched on an ancient trunk, their eyes tracking us as we approached.

"This is all the old stuff that was here when I was a little girl." Millie looked around at the piled-up junk. This section did appear to have items that were much older... and much more deteriorated.

"The trunk looks ancient." The cats hopped off as I approached. They stood at my feet, looking up at me as if encouraging me to open it. If I had any doubts before that the cats were trying to communicate, I didn't now.

"That's a steamer trunk," Mom said. "For going on ships. Very old."

"It must have belonged to Jedediah Biddeford!" Millie lifted the top. It creaked and groaned as she pulled it up gently.

"Are you thinking what I'm thinking?" Mom said as she peered in.

"The old buckle." Millie reached in and started pushing the items aside. The smell of mildew wafted up and I sneezed again.

The trunk contained old clothing and personal items. Mom gingerly held up the shoulders of a disintegrating tweed suit. "This looks like the suit Jed was wearing in that drawing. You know, the one in the Oyster Cove history book."

Millie glanced at the suit. "It sure does. And if that's in here, maybe those shoes are in here. And if the shoes are in here… are the buckles with them or is one missing?"

We carefully moved the items aside. No shoes.

"No shoes. No buckles." Millie looked excited. "Do you think this is where the killer got the buckle from?"

"Who had been up here?" Mom asked.

"Ed said he heard someone and thought it was Anita Pendragon." I glanced around at the dusty attic floor. "But…"

"Any of the guests could have snuck up here, though," Millie said.

"Wait, something isn't right." I swiped my finger through the thick layer of dust on an oak table that sat beside the trunk. "The floor was covered in dust when we came up. The only thing disturbing the path to this trunk was the cats' paw prints. I remember looking at them."

We all looked back toward the path, which of course was now marred with our own footprints. "There's another path from the corner there." Millie pointed to a row of furniture and boxes, which had been pushed aside to form a narrow path, but it had a layer of undisturbed dust. "Hmmm, no footprints there. So how would someone have gotten to the trunk?"

"They couldn't. Not unless they hopped across the furniture," I said.

"Or floated over like a ghost." Mom glanced around the room as if expecting one.

"There is no ghost." Millie closed the trunk. "The shoes and buckle were probably never in here. We don't know for sure that the buckle on Madame Zenda was actually Jed's. I'm sure there are other old buckles that look like his. Now let's get a move on, we have suspects to scrutinize. This buckle angle is a dead end."

Meow! Nero hopped up on the trunk and cast an accusatory glare at Millie.

Meroo! Marlowe weaved on the path in front of us.

"I know you guys mean well." Millie picked up steam as we neared the attic door. "But I'm not sure what you wanted to tell us. We already know this is all about the psychics pretending they are talking to Jed. Is that what you were trying to tell us?"

Meoooo.

Meope.

Millie ignored the cats' meows as we funneled out onto the second-floor landing. Flora was there, dusting a bench that sat underneath the window. She gave our dusty clothes a look of disapproval and then tried to dust Mom off with her feather duster.

"What have you people been doing up in the attic? It's dirty up there and I have enough work as it is," Flora said.

"We were just looking for something." Millie pushed the duster away as Flora turned it on her.

"Well, I hope you don't expect me to clean up there. I don't do attics. Hard enough to keep the regular house clean. And I hope you don't expect me to be cleaning the outbuildings either," Flora huffed.

"Outbuildings?" I asked.

Flora nodded. "And don't you listen to any of those crazy guests either. I keep the bathrooms clean as a whistle. I don't know why that crystal ball lady thinks she needed to resort to using the outhouse."

"Esther? You saw her in the outhouse?" Mom raised her brows at me. "Is that where you saw her, Josie?"

"No, I saw her near the barn. That's pretty far away." I turned to Flora. "Are you sure you saw her in there?"

"Do you think I'm blind?" Flora pushed the thick glasses up on her nose. "Just because I wear these doesn't mean I can't see. Like right now, I can see Myron Remington as plain as day."

We all swiveled to look out the window. Flora was right. Myron was standing by the side of an old shed. He was looking around as if assessing the grounds. My gut clenched. Why would he be doing that? It was almost as if he were scoping out the place, trying to figure out what he would do with the property when he seized it for non-payment of the loan. I could just imagine visions of condos or a strip mall dancing through his head.

Mom, Millie and I clustered around the small window, watching as he looked out toward the ocean, then back at the shed. We jumped back when his gaze drifted to the house.

"What is he doing out there?" Mom asked.

"Looks like he's checking out the grounds. Maybe he thinks you need to get the landscaping done, Josie," Millie said.

"Maybe." I hoped that was all it was, but the way he was looking around I didn't think so.

"Well, I don't like him showing up here all the time. I mean, it's not like he bought the place, he just gave you a loan. I have a good mind to run down there and tell him so."

Millie started toward the door, but I put my hand on her arm to hold her back.

"Maybe it's better if we just let him go about his business. This will all blow over after the killer is caught and these guests figure out they can't talk to Jed." I hoped.

Millie sighed. "Fine. I suppose you're right. All the more reason for us to figure out who the killer is before Myron comes up with a reason to renege on the loan."

"Don't let him get mud in here." Flora's glasses reflected light from the window as she turned to me. "I just spent a good hour cleaning up the mud one of them traipsed in. It's enough cleaning up after the guests, but you need to do something about keeping the whole town from traipsing in!"

The whole town? "I'm sorry about that, but Myron did give me a loan and I want to stay on his good side."

"Yeah him too, but he's not the one who traipsed mud in the back entry. That was a mess to clean up," Flora said.

"Well then who did?" Millie asked.

"Anita Pendragon. You ask me, that nosey reporter is up to something."

Marlowe rolled her eyes at the backs of Josie, Rose and Millie as they exited the attic. "I guess they didn't get our drift."

"Don't be too harsh," Nero said. "Josie did understand we wanted her up here. They just didn't get the part about the shoes being missing."

Marlowe sighed. "I suppose we can't expect too much. They don't have our superior skills of deduction so wouldn't know the shoes had been there."

"To be fair, we did have Jed to tell us that. I'm not sure we would have figured that out on our own, either." Nero secretly enjoyed putting Marlowe in her place sometimes, but fair was fair. *He* might have been able to sniff out the fact that the shoes had once been in there, but he was sure Marlowe wouldn't have. But without Jed to lead them up here and tell them about the shoes, he was certain that he wouldn't have even thought of it.

"I don't know about that Josie. She seems a little dense." Jed tapped the side of his head. "Doesn't catch on fast and she didn't even lock the door when they left. Not like my girl, Esther. Now that one's a keeper. Much nicer than that shrew I married."

Jed's face got all pinched, apparently with memories of his dead wife. Was he wondering if the shrew had killed him? If she had, could Nero prove that somehow? He glanced around at the stacks of boxes and papers. Maybe the murder weapon was in one of these boxes and he could sniff it out. Or there might be an article in one of the papers showing Helena Biddeford unusually happy after her husband's death.

"It's still a bust. As Josie said, there were no footprints going to the trunk, so who could have taken the shoes?" Marlowe's words dragged Nero back to the present. They had a more important murder to solve right now. Jed's murder could wait.

"Maybe they were clever enough not to leave footprints." Nero studied the furniture in the attic. Someone *could* have traversed a path to the trunk without leaving footprints, he supposed.

"The guests here *are* a sneaky bunch. I think we have a bit more investigating to do. The buckle is a dead end." Marlowe fluffed her tail. "Get it? *Dead* end."

"But how would they do that? Levitate?" Nero had heard of things like levitation and astral projection and he'd seen Victor meditating, but his butt had always been planted firmly on the chair.

"Guess we need to find that out," Marlowe said.

Jed had swirled over to the window and was dripping ectoplasm on the floor. "I saw that mean banker skulking around out there. I don't much like him. He worries Josie and I don't want her to worry. Maybe I should haunt him."

"Not a bad idea." Nero smiled at the thought of Myron being haunted, especially since Myron seemed to be getting worked up about all the ghost talk.

Jed tapped his fingers on his lips. "I think I have an idea that can help out Josie, and my beautiful Esther, plus give Myron the shaft."

Nero perked up. "I like that idea. Will it help find the killer?"

"Whose? Mine or that tarot reader's?"

"Either."

"Maybe not. But I'm not really all that keen on finding my killer anymore. Since I've been communicating with Esther my feelings about moving on to the afterlife have changed." Jed got all dreamy looking and his normally white ghostly image turned pink.

"Yech," Marlowe said.

Nero agreed, but at least Jed wasn't fixated on Josie anymore. If he attached himself to Esther and wanted to stay on the earthly plane, then he'd be leaving when Esther did and that was just fine with Nero.

"So, what are you going to do that will help Josie and Esther and annoy Myron?" Marlowe asked.

"Not sure exactly yet. I'm working on a plan, though," Jed said.

"Speaking of annoying Myron and working on a plan, we need to do both." Nero hopped down from the old Eastlake bureau he'd been sitting on so he could look out the window. "I say we start with annoying Myron. He hates getting cat hair on his nice slacks. Let's go find him before he leaves and rub up against the bottom of his pants."

Chapter Eighteen

Mom and Millie headed off to the police station to try to wheedle some more information out of Seth Chamberlain. I stayed behind to catch up on household chores. I kept an eye out the window for Anita Pendragon. She was up to something and I wanted to catch her in the act. It took a few hours, but luck was with me. I was at the kitchen sink washing dishes when I saw her peeking out from behind a lilac bush. I hurried out to catch her at whatever it was she was up to.

I picked my way along the side of the house, my back pressed to the paint-peeling clapboards as I used the house for cover. I was at the back of the building and hadn't gotten around to scraping and painting the exterior here yet since it wasn't visible to the guests.

I came to the corner and quickly darted over, taking refuge behind a giant rhododendron. Peering out from behind the glossy leaves, I watched Anita as the floral smell of summer flowers wafted over. Out here in back of the house only the hum of buzzing bees broke the silence.

Anita appeared to be scoping out the grounds. What on earth was she doing? I had news for her too, her lime-green-and-turquoise shirt did little to camouflage her behind the dark green shrub.

I snuck up behind her very quietly and when I was within two feet I said, "Aha!"

Anita whirled around dropping her navy-blue tote bag as her hands flew to her heart. Once she recognized me her eyes narrowed to slits. "Josie... Waters... what in the world are you doing... scaring me like that!"

The nerve of her yelling at me! "What are *you* doing lurking in my bushes?"

Anita recovered from her scare. Now she looked angry instead of startled. Smoothing down the bottom of her shirt, she said, "It's a free country."

"Not quite, this is private property."

"Okay, fine. I'm here doing investigatory journalism. There was a murder here, you know. And a ghost is running about. The people have a right to know."

"Why does that necessitate lurking around in my yard?"

She leaned toward me, lowering her voice. "Your guests aren't the most innocent of people. They're suspects, you know. And besides, they get up to some strange things. Seances in outhouses and convening with spirits in gazebos."

I had seen some of the guests skulking around in the yard, but seances and spirit communications? "Are you sure they've been doing that?"

"I'm not sure what they're up to, but whatever it is, I'm getting the scoop." Anita crossed her arms over her chest and adopted a bit of attitude. "You might thank me for that. It's down to my investigating out here that I found Madame Zenda's body. If I hadn't come by, there's no telling how long she would have been moldering out there."

Found her there or *put* her there? I didn't want to rile Anita up any more than she already was so I kept silent, scowling at her with my hand on my hips. I figured I'd let her talk and maybe she'd incriminate herself.

My silence must have unnerved her. She looked away. "Mark my words, someone in this guesthouse is up to something."

"Yeah and I think it's *you*."

Anita jerked back. "Me? What are you talking about? I'm just reporting what people need to know and if it happens to be a good story that sells, well then, what's wrong with that?" She looked at me out of the corner of her eye. "I don't see why you're so upset about it. Unless you have something to hide, like the fact that you're a killer."

Now it was my turn to get upset. "Why would I kill Madame Zenda?"

"It would make for good publicity. Come to think of it, you've had a couple of murders here. And didn't the discovery of the skeleton bring you the guests you have now? This would make a good story. The black-widow guesthouse owner who kills her guests."

"Now wait just a minute, I didn't kill anyone! I helped catch the first two killers and now I'm going to catch this one. Which brings me to my question: Why did you break into the guesthouse?"

"Break in? What are you talking about?" She looked away. "I've never been in there."

Now I knew she was lying. Could she really be the killer? And if so, maybe it was dangerous to confront her like this. But my brain must have been a few seconds behind my mouth because the words came out before I stopped to think about the safest course of action. "Ed saw you peeking in the window and said you might have been in the house, and Flora said you tracked mud into the back foyer. Now, why would you lie about that if you weren't the killer?" I got my cell phone out of my pocket. "I'm calling Sheriff Chamberlain."

"No wait!" She shifted on her feet, her eyes darting from the house to me. "Okay. Fine. I *was* in the guesthouse but not because I'm the killer. As I've told you, I'm working on a story. There might be a movie deal and… well… I needed an insider so I could get a scoop on what was really going on."

"Madame Zenda?"

"Yeah, at first. She was my contact."

That explained the open windows.

"That's why I was the one who found her. She was going to talk to Jedediah Biddeford that night." Anita chewed her bottom lip. "Though to tell the truth, I think she might have been a fraud. Anyway, she wouldn't tell me exactly where and I was trying to figure that out so I could see the communication, but instead I saw her body. She was dead when I got there."

"And you didn't see the killer leaving or hear anything?" I was dubious.

She shook her head. "I wish. That would have made a great headline. 'Reporter Captures Killer.' But I didn't see a thing. Of course, I was a bit freaked out, what with her lying there. I didn't kill her though. Why would I? She was my contact."

Anita's explanation made sense and, given that she was calmly discussing this instead of trying to kill me, my feeling that she was the killer was waning. But Flora had said she'd been in the house *after* Madame Zenda was killed. If Zenda was her contact, then what was she doing in there? Hiding evidence?

"Then why were you in the guesthouse after she was killed?"

Anita sighed. "Fine. I'll tell you. I was meeting Victor Merino." My left brow quirked up. "Why?"

"I've sort of teamed up with him for the story. There's a lot riding on it."

"So, let me get this straight. You were teamed up with Madame Zenda and then, after she died, you teamed up with Victor. How? Did you already know him?" What if Victor had killed Madame Zenda because he wanted the fame and knew that Anita could help him get it?

She shook her head. "I didn't know him. He saw me talking to that movie producer downtown and asked me all sorts of questions. I guess he already knew about the movie. Anyway, he suggested we combine forces."

"Combine forces? How?"

"He was going to feed me information. That's why I met him in the foyer the other day and why I'm here now. He said something is about to happen." Anita glanced out over the yard. "But I'm not so sure I believe him."

"Did he say *what* was going to happen?" I didn't like the ominous way that sounded, but then Victor did seem to be overly dramatic. "I think sometimes he exaggerates."

"Yeah, that's why I'm out here to follow him, just in case."

I peered into the dense overgrowth of the yard. "He's out here?"

"No. The only one I've seen is that weird tea-leaf reader."

"Gail? Why do you say she's weird?" I thought she was weird too, but wanted to know Anita's reasons.

"No background." At my curious look Anita stood straighter. "I've done background checks on all these people. They're all mediums who have businesses and a history. All except Gail. Not even a classified ad back in her paper in Ohio. And the other day when I was talking to the movie producer and ran into Victor, guess who I saw watching us?"

"Gail?"

"Yep."

I'd seen Gail watching Victor too. At least that's what I thought she'd been doing when I'd run into her looking for tea in the pantry. But why watch Victor? If she'd seen him with the movie producer, then she knew about the potential movie. Was she trying to steal the limelight from Victor somehow? But why not just claim she could talk to Jed herself? If she did that, then the attention would be on her. Instead, she was hiding and following people.

"What do you think she's up to?" I asked.

"Beats me." Anita bent down to pick up the tote bag she'd dropped when I'd startled her. The bag spilled over and a copy of the early etching of the guesthouse with Jed Biddeford and family tumbled out.

My eyes went right to the buckle on his shoes. Anita knew about the buckle. My eyes flicked to hers, a shiver running through me. I grabbed the paper, noticing another one behind it. This other one was of Jedediah Biddeford signing something. He had a fancy carved-ivory quill pen in his hand. Why did she have these drawings of Jed? Was she scoping out Jed's belongings? Maybe planning to leave another piece of memorabilia on her next body?

"Aha! You have a photograph of the drawing of Jed's buckle!" I pointed to the shoe in the photo.

Anita tried to snatch the papers away, but I pulled them out of her hands. She sighed and crossed her arms over her chest. "Of course I have images of Jed. Like I just told you, I do my research. I looked up all kinds of things about the family."

"Why would you need to do that? Seems like a lot of work," I said.

"Not really. They have all this stuff down at the bank. There's a whole display of Remington memorabilia and since the Biddefords were big in town back then, there's a lot of images of the Oyster Cove Guesthouse and Jedediah Biddeford too."

I usually did my banking online but now I remembered the display down at the bank. It was off to one side and included all kinds of things like the bank's first coin, etchings of the original bank—an old shack complete with iron bars—various old desk implements, pens, bank notes and so on.

"Do they have personal items there?" I was thinking about the shoes.

Anita grabbed for the papers again and this time I let her take them. They crinkled as she shoved them in her tote bag.

"Personal items? I'm not sure. I mean, they have an old inkwell and a desk blotter that they first used in the bank. It's kind of like a mini museum."

It was probably a long shot, but what if the killer got the buckle from the bank? Some of it was locked up, some of it was out in the open. If the shoes with the buckle had been there, would the killer have been able to swipe it without anyone noticing? This didn't let Anita off the hook, she'd been there and knew what was in the collection. Would she be dumb enough to admit that to me now, though? Probably not.

Suddenly I had the urge to make a deposit at the bank. I wanted to see exactly what was in that display... or, more importantly, to see if anything was missing.

Chapter Nineteen

I rushed in the back door and down the hallway on the way to my car, which was parked out front. I didn't make it to the door though because a heated argument was brewing in the parlor.

"I call foul on that! If you talked to Jedediah Biddeford, then I'm a monkey's uncle." Esther's voice reached me in the hallway and I looked into the parlor to see her looking down at Victor, her hands on her hips and a scowl on her face.

"I'm telling you the truth!" Victor was wearing a gray velour jogging suit. He patted his mustache and looked up at Esther innocently. "Jed will talk to me tonight. We'll find the treasure and he will give me a unique clue to solve his murder."

"Ha! That's how I know you're lying." Esther leaned down toward Victor. "There is no treasure."

"How do you know that?" Victor fixed her with a shrewd gaze.

Esther frowned. "I… Umm… Well, after all these years it's doubtful. And I read that there was a big treasure hunt here a few weeks ago. Nothing was found."

"We'll see about that." Victor shifted in his chair, noticing me in the doorway. "Your guesthouse will be famous. Especially when they make the movie."

"Movie?" Gail, who was on the sofa and had been gazing into a dainty floral teacup looked up at him. "What movie?"

"Yeah, what movie?" Esther echoed.

Victor made a face at Esther. "Don't give me that. I saw you in town. You know that there is a movie producer sniffing around the story of Jedediah Biddeford's skeleton. And he is well aware that I am the only real psychic here."

"Madame Zenda claimed that she was going to talk to Jed's ghost too and look what happened to her," Gail said.

Something flickered across Victor's face. Guilt over killing Madame Zenda or fear that the same thing would happen to him?

Esther spun on her heel and went to sit in front of her crystal ball. It was on the table next to the window and the sunlight filtering in made the ball glow with an eerie light. She passed her hands over it and closed her eyes. "I don't think Jed would like having his story sensationalized in a movie and I doubt he has any good clues as to who his killer is. And good luck with that treasure!"

Victor waved a hand at her. "We'll see tonight. I think I will pick an interesting setting. Like maybe the old family graveyard or that spooky gazebo. It's important to set the ambiance, you know how movie people are all about that sort of thing."

Esther glared at him. Gail went back to gazing at her teacup. I turned and left to go to the bank.

I didn't know whether or not Victor was really going to talk to Jed, but he was right about one thing. *Something* was going to happen tonight. I hoped there would be a clue to this whole thing at the bank.

Because if Victor was the killer, I had no intention of letting him get a movie deal with his fake communication with Jed. And if he wasn't the killer... then I was afraid he might be the next victim.

It was late afternoon when I got to the bank. The free cookies at the teller window reminded me that I had to start thinking about tomorrow's breakfast. Millie would have a fit if I didn't have something in mind. I grabbed a cookie—chocolate chip—and headed toward the back of the bank where the display was located.

The area wasn't large, just a case built in to the wall and a roped-off area where an old oak rolltop desk sat. On top of the desk was a brass lamp with a green shade, an inkwell and an old silver pen atop a desk blotter. An antique brass-and-black-enamel sign for the teller window sat off to one side, along with the old-fashioned window complete with iron bars and frosted glass.

The locked case had interesting old coins, many of which weren't even used for currency today. Myron sold old silver dollars and other old and rare coins at the bank, but the ones in the case were much older.

The wall beside the case had a pictorial display of town history. The etching of Jed that Anita had was there, along with other drawings and old grainy photos of the bank along with the changes to the building over the centuries. On the end was a copy of the old etching of the Oyster Cove Guesthouse highlighting the connection between the Remingtons and the Biddefords and Thomas Remington's humble beginnings as Jed's butler. I turned away, depressed. There were no old clothes. Maybe another cookie would perk me up.

But before I could make another trip past the plate of cookies, Myron stepped in my path. Perfect, as if the trip wasn't a downer before, now I had to deal with him.

"Josie, what brings you here? Your loan payment isn't due until the thirtieth." Myron smiled at me, but I could tell it was fake.

"I know. I was just… um… checking my balance." I certainly didn't want him to know about my suspicions. He was already acting strangely enough as it was, no need to remind him of the unsavory happenings at the guesthouse.

Myron's brows tugged together. "Don't you do that online?"

"Sometimes. Hey, speaking of wondering why someone is at a certain place, why were you at the guesthouse earlier today?"

Myron looked taken aback. "What are you talking about? I didn't see you at the guesthouse earlier."

"You were out on the grounds. Near the barn and overgrown gardens."

Myron glanced around the lobby, probably making sure no one overheard the awkward conversation. He was all about keeping up appearances, which was probably the reason why he was so bothered by the ghost business at the guesthouse. And the murders... though I suppose anyone would be bothered by that.

"Not sure what you're talking about," Myron said.

I looked down to see cat hair on the cuffs of his pants. There were little black ones mixed with brown and white. Nero and Marlowe? Usually Myron was very fastidious about his appearance, so if the cats had rubbed against him when he'd been there earlier, surely he would have cleaned the hairs off by now. The cats couldn't possibly be in the bank, could they?

"Speaking of the grounds." Myron lowered his voice. "I spoke with Mike Sullivan about the gazebo and you'll have to watch out that people don't go out to that ramshackle thing before it's fixed properly. Wouldn't want a lawsuit. That would be grounds to terminate the loan. I may have to inspect that thing myself when Mike takes a look at it later."

Ed would start work on the gazebo shortly and I vaguely remembered Mike saying something about coming out to inspect the gazebo for the permit. Had Mike said something about it to Myron? I was skeptical, as I was pretty sure that if something was wrong, Mike would have mentioned it to me first. I didn't think guests were in the habit of going to the gazebo anyway, but even so, Myron was probably making something out of nothing. Which made me wonder if that was why he'd been out there earlier in the first place. Was he looking for a reason to call in the loan?

I was about to ask when Rita Fortin came into the lobby. She was from a wealthy family and liked to flaunt it with designer outfits and purses that cost as much as a compact car. Today was no exception. She scanned the lobby from behind overly large sunglasses, her gaze stopping when it fell on Myron. Always one to follow the money, Myron immediately hurried over to suck up to her without so much as a goodbye to me.

It was just as well, what I had been about to say to him wasn't very nice. Better to have some time to cool off before I got Myron riled up. After all, he did hold my future in his hands.

As Myron ushered Rita into his office, Belinda May, one of the tellers, started toward me, shooting looks over her shoulder at Myron to make sure he didn't notice.

"Hey, Josie, I have this for one of your guests. I was wondering if you could take it back for them. I was supposed to meet them later today, but my grandmother is ill and I can't." She held a plain A4 manila envelope out to me.

"You want me to give this to Victor?" I mean, I assumed it was him since he was the one with an agenda. The envelope had no name on it.

"No. Esther. That nice crystal-ball lady."

"She was here?" I looked back at the display area then down at the envelope, remembering how upset Esther had been at Victor's pronouncement.

Belinda glanced around as if to make sure no one could overhear. "She was looking at the memorabilia area, then she gave me a lovely reading with her crystal ball. Of course, Myron wasn't here then. I do hope her readings are true. She said a silver-haired fox would sweep me off my feet."

"She did, did she?" I shook the envelope. Nothing rattled. "So, what's in the envelope?"

"Oh, just some information about the bank's history."

"Why would she want that?" I felt along the envelope, expecting to feel the bulk of a buckle or button or something, but it was flat. Just paper.

Belinda shrugged. "I guess she found it interesting. Don't worry, it's nothing confidential. I mean, I'm sure it's okay to give out, but you know how Myron can be… speaking of that, I need to get back to my station."

She rushed off, leaving me staring at the envelope. I was dying to know what was in it and why Esther would want information on the bank's history, but it was sealed. Did I dare open it? I wasn't sure I wanted to tip off Esther to the fact that I'd seen the contents. Which left me wondering… what in the world was Esther up to?

🐾

Nero sniffed the contents of the Styrofoam container that Harry had pilfered from the dumpster of the Marinara Mariner. Red sauce, linguini… ahhh… there was a morsel of succulent shrimp. Nero gobbled it up and then licked his paws, washing his white tuxedo to remove any evidence of sauce.

"No squid-ink dish today." Juliette hopped down from the rim of the dumpster and eyed the container in front of Nero. "The only thing in here is common food, unfortunately."

"Indeed." Boots sniffed the air with disdain.

Nero had to admit, it was smelly here in the alley beside the restaurant. But sometimes Tony left good scraps for them and it was worth a try. Besides, they had an ulterior motive to meet there, it was across from the bank and they'd been watching Myron ever since Marlowe and Nero had seen him at the guesthouse.

"Myron hasn't left the bank since we started the stakeout." Stubbs' voice wafted up from the dumpster. "Speaking of which, I wish Tony had put some steak out."

"What's going on with the police?" Nero asked Harry.

"According to Louie, Millie and Rose came to the station and tried to get information out of Seth but he clammed up," Harry said.

"Clam sauce? Don't think so. I don't smell any in here!" Stubbs yelled from the dumpster.

Harry gave the dumpster the side-eye. "Would you come out of there, there's nothing good inside."

"Fine." Stubbs appeared on the rim, then jumped down shaking the dumpster debris off his orange coat.

"So, as I was saying," Harry continued, "Seth didn't tell much to Rose and Millie, but Louie said that they are narrowing things down to one suspect."

"Who?" Juliette asked.

"He didn't know. They are being very hush-hush."

"I bet it's that guy with the mustache." Boots glanced over at the bank. "He was in the bank earlier."

"You mean the man with the soft suits who is staying at the guesthouse? The one who came to the rectory?" Juliette asked.

Boots nodded.

"Victor," Nero said. "Did he do anything suspicious?"

"He came out of the bank with a burlap bag. He was glancing all around and then hopped into an Uber."

"What was in the bag?" Marlowe asked.

"How big was it?" Stubbs added.

"No idea what was in it," Boots said. "It was about the size of an old bag of marbles and looked like it had something of heft and weight in it."

"Why would Victor want marbles?" Harry asked.

"I didn't say it *was* marbles." Boots narrowed his eyes and looked toward the bank as if trying to visualize Victor and the burlap bag. "Just looked like something heavy."

"Huh, well that bears investigating." Nero looked at Marlowe. "Perhaps we should head back to the guesthouse and see what our velour-wearing guest is up to."

"You might want to hurry." Juliette swished her tail ominously. "That movie producer came to visit Father Tim again and he's leaving town tomorrow. If the reason for the murder was to gain fame with a movie, whoever is behind it might be trying to step up their game."

Chapter Twenty

I found Esther in the front parlor. Good thing she was alone, maybe I could get her to tell me what the contents of the envelope were. Then again, maybe it wasn't a good thing to be alone with her if she was the killer.

Nero and Marlowe were sitting on her lap. As I got closer, I could see she was feeding them some kind of treat. They didn't seem bothered at all that she might be a killer, I could hear their purrs out in the hallway. Those furry little traitors would go to anyone for treats, yet when I put their dishes down with their nutritious cat food in it, they circled, sniffed and looked at me suspiciously as if I was trying to poison them.

Esther and the cats looked up as I approached. I gave Nero and Marlowe the stink-eye but they both just blinked at me with blank expressions.

I thrust the envelope out at her. "Just what is this?"

Meow. Nero sniffed the envelope and then squinted at me.

"You tell me." She took the envelope cautiously. Playing dumb, was she? "Where did you get this?"

I fisted my hands on my hips. "Belinda at the bank gave it to me."

Marlowe hopped on the table and stretched out to head-butt my hand. I relaxed and petted her soft head. At least there was one cat who knew which side to be on. Nero remained in Esther's lap.

"Oh…" Esther put the envelope aside. "That Belinda sure is nice. This is just some research I had her do for me."

"Research? On what?"

She glanced at the crystal ball and it sparked, attracting the cats' attention. They batted it gently with their paws.

"You'll have to wait and see about that. I can tell you one thing, that Victor isn't going to get away with stealing the show this time."

I didn't know what to make of this. Esther was acting more like a kindly old lady than a killer, but maybe she was good at pretending. I was mulling over how to approach my interrogation when the sound of tires on the driveway caught my attention.

Mom and Millie were pulling to a stop and right behind them was Mike and then behind him was Myron.

Ughh. What was Myron doing here? It wasn't even an hour ago that he'd been schmoozing with Rita Fortin at the bank. Maybe he was coming to scope out a location for the pool for the condos he'd build once he foreclosed on the loan? I know he'd said he was going to have Mike show him the gazebo at some point, but this soon? I wondered if he had ulterior motives. At least now I'd have backup if Esther tried anything. Though she didn't seem like she was going to attack. She was simply sitting calmly in her chair, the cats back in her lap as if she had nothing to hide.

I stepped out into the foyer as Mom and Millie came through the door. Flora was dusting the Tiffany glass lamp on the round mahogany table, apparently oblivious to our new arrivals.

"Oh, Josie, there you are. We just came from the sheriff's office," Millie said, glancing behind her as Mike and then Myron piled into the foyer.

"And?" I asked.

Millie looked deflated. "Nothing new on the case, but we ran into Mike there. He was coming here anyway so he followed us."

Mike smiled. "Hey, Sunshine."

"Hi. What brings you here?" Mike and Myron were starting to frequent the guesthouse as much as Millie and Mom did.

He held up the clipboard that was in his hand and tapped it with a pencil. "Permit for the gazebo, remember?"

I glanced at Myron at the mention of the gazebo. Mike had issued the permit so that was a good thing, right?

"I came because of the gazebo, too," Myron said.

Mike frowned at him. "I hardly think that's necessary. I wasn't talking about much of anything, anyway. Ed can move forward with the work." He raised a brow at me and handed me the permit.

Millie leveled a look at Myron. "Now, Myron, don't you think you are getting a little too involved in the business here? Why, barely a day passes when you don't stop by."

Myron looked affronted. "Well, it *is* my investment."

Mom clacked her tongue against the roof of her mouth. "Myron, look here. I know you have a crush on Josie but really your excuses to come here are growing quite thin."

"And of no use," Esther piped in from the parlor. "Remember, the ball showed tall, dark and handsome." She shot me a knowing glance before casting an approving look in Mike's direction.

Myron straightened the cuffs of his expensive gray suit. "As charming as Josie is, she is *not* the reason I come here. She's a client, nothing more. It's just that the bank wants to foster community ties. And with the Oyster Cove Guesthouse being such an important part of Oyster Cove history, I feel I have a duty to see it restored back to its former glory." He leaned in and lowered his voice, although why he felt like he had to do that was beyond me, it wasn't like there was anyone else in the foyer. "It's good for business if the customers know that you have pride in your own community."

"If you've come for the show, you're all too early. That won't be until ten p.m." Victor strode down the hall. This time he was wearing a white golf shirt and tan khaki pants. I had to do a double take as I'd never seen him in anything but his velour jogging suits. "It seems ghosts like to operate under the cover of darkness."

"Show?" Mike shot me a quizzical look.

Esther pushed up from the table, dislodging the cats who thudded to the floor. "Mr. Big Shot thinks that he's going to talk to Jedediah Biddeford, but I have it on good authority that Jed won't be speaking to him. And there *is* no treasure. Jed doesn't need anyone making a mockery of him. But if his killer can be found, then I will be the one to do that, not Victor."

"We'll see about that." Victor puffed up, his tone imbued with the utmost confidence. "I think the discovery of the treasure might make me famous."

Millie huffed. "Good luck with that. The previous guests dug up the yard looking, along with half the town. Besides, there is no ghost."

Thud!

We whirled around to see a Staffordshire figurine of a shepherdess with a baby lamb had fallen off the table. Lucky thing it had landed on the red-and-navy oriental carpet or it would have been in pieces. The cats were circling it sniffing and looking up at the table.

"That's odd." Millie picked it up and inspected it for damage. "I wonder how that—"

"*WOOOOHOOOOAAAANNN…*"

The eerie sound drifted through the air, freezing us all in our tracks. Even the cats seemed startled, cocking their heads to one side as if to try to determine what the strange noise was.

"*OOOOHGAAAAAAAHHHH…*"

"What the heck is that?" Mike asked.

"Is it the pipes?" I ventured, because what else could be making that ungodly noise?

"Sorry, Sunshine, that's not the sound of any pipes I've ever heard."

We were all silent, waiting to hear more, but not a sound came. I thought I could hear Myron whimpering behind Mom and Millie.

"You don't think it really could be a ghost?" Mom asked.

Flora, who had been dusting the top of the newel post, turned around, holding the duster feather side up. "If you've got a ghost, I hope you don't expect me to clean up after it. I don't do ectoplasmic goo. That stuff is hard to get out of linens."

"Don't be silly. There must be a reasonable explanation..." Millie glanced up at the ceiling as if expecting to see a ghost floating around up there.

Esther crossed her arms over her chest and turned to Victor. "Maybe it's Jed. Perhaps he'd like to speak to you now. Go ahead, talk to him. Enlighten us as to what he wants."

"Uhh... that wasn't the plan. I'm sure it's not Jed." Victor sounded nervous.

"You mean there might be two ghosts?" Mom asked. Surely she was joking. She didn't really believe there was a ghost in the Oyster Cove Guesthouse, let alone two of them?

Myron peeked out from behind Mom and Millie. His eyes were as big as the old silver dollars he sold for a premium down at the bank, his shoulders were rounded and his hands stuffed in his pockets as if he were trying to become even smaller than he already was. He was probably hoping the ghost wouldn't notice him and pick on one of us instead.

"A real ghost..." he managed to utter as he glanced at the grandfather clock in the corner. "Hmmm, look at the time. Guess I can't go look at the gazebo after all. Gotta run!"

We all watched as he dashed out the door.

Ghost or not, Myron was spooked. This did not bode well for the guesthouse at all.

Chapter Twenty-One

Nero eyed Jed. "Really, don't you think the ghostly moans are a bit much?"

"I beg your pardon." Jed swirled indignantly. "That wasn't me. You think I'd stoop to those sorts of theatrics, do you? No self-respecting ghost would make noises like that."

"You did push the figurine off. I saw you," Marlowe said.

Jed crossed his arms over his chest. "That's because that pompous bore Victor was arguing with my Esther."

"*Your* Esther?" Maybe Jed was getting a little too attached to Esther. "Well, I don't want to presume, but we have had some lovely conversations through her crystal ball. I think she really cares for me." Jed got all moony-eyed and Nero tried to steer the conversation in a more productive direction.

"If it wasn't you, then who was it?"

"Probably that fraud Victor trying to sensationalize things for that producer. He was out by the gazebo earlier." Jed's expression turned pensive. "Is that where the sound came from? Maybe he was hiding something out there that could produce sound? I know you have all sorts of devices in this day and age and I've heard sound come out of that small box Josie always seems to have in her hand."

"Her phone?" Nero asked.

"If that's what you call it," Jed said. "Anyway, wouldn't be hard to have something make those sounds. Someone should tell the person that ghosts don't actually sound like that, though."

"So it's not another ghost?" Marlowe sounded relieved.

"Of course not. If another ghost were here, I'd know," Jed said.

"What about your wife?" Nero asked. He hadn't fully dismissed the idea that she might have come here for some sort of revenge on Jed, but it didn't really add up. Why would she wait all this time and why try to frame him for killing Madame Zenda? He was already dead so nothing would happen to him. No, it was more likely the culprit was of the human form.

"My wife?" Jed ducked behind a chair. "You haven't seen her here, have you? I don't want to run into her."

"Haven't seen her," Nero said. "Thought maybe you could sense her."

"Thankfully not. That woman might have done me in. Though I think we'll find out about that soon."

"We will?" Marlowe asked.

Jed looked uncertain. "Maybe. Then again, maybe I don't want to know who killed me. I might just want to stick around on this plane." Jed sent a lovesick glance at Esther who was walking back to the table with her crystal ball. The group of humans were splitting up. Victor was heading upstairs to his room and Rose, Millie, Josie and Mike looked to be heading to the kitchen. It appeared as if everyone in the house was going about their business, despite the ghostly sounds. Wait… not everyone. Someone was missing.

"Where is Gail Weathers?" Nero asked.

"The tea-leaf lady?" Marlowe glanced around. "Don't know. She wasn't here when we heard the sounds."

Nero looked at Jed. "You haven't seen her around the place in your ghostly travels, have you?"

Jed shook his head. "Nope. Been busy watching over Esther. She's getting my communication nicely now and let's just say she might scratch my back if I'll scratch hers."

"Ohh, that sounds lovely." Marlowe scratched at her ear. "Summertime can be very itchy, what with the pesky gnats and all."

Nero didn't take Jed's words so literally. It sounded like Jed was up to something and Nero wasn't sure he would like it. "What do you mean by that?"

"Don't you go getting your whiskers in a bunch. Josie will benefit from it too," Jed said. "Now, about that Gail Weathers. Isn't she the one who always has a cup in her hand? I did see her out at the gazebo earlier today, shortly after Victor made that ridiculous announcement."

Nero and Marlowe exchanged a glance.

"Do you think the noises could have come from the gazebo?" Marlowe asked.

Nero bestowed a fond look on the young cat. She might be prone to jumping to conclusions, like thinking there was a second ghost, but she was picking up the clues nicely. "I do think it could have. Looks like we better get out there and investigate."

Millie's ample back end stuck out of the fridge as she rummaged for food. "If I was going to fake a ghost, I'd do a much better job than that clichéd moaning."

"Well, it scared Myron. He ran out of here like his pants were on fire." Mom pulled a box of crackers out of the cabinet. "Come to think of it, that might not have been such a bad thing if his pants did burn. Did you see all the cat hair on his cuffs?"

The fact that Myron had run out like that made me nervous. Apparently he was terrified of ghosts. Now it made sense that he'd been making a big deal about the ghost affecting the financial future of the guesthouse. "I just hope he didn't run straight to the bank to rip up my loan papers."

Millie backed out of the fridge with a handful of various cheeses. "Now, don't you worry about him. I know his grandmother and if he does anything to hurt the guesthouse I'll have her give him a talking to."

I doubted Myron would keep the loan on his grandmother's say-so, but at least that was something.

"He wouldn't take the loan away, would he?" Mike's velvety eyes were oozing with sympathy, which made me feel all funny inside.

I looked away. "I don't know, but if he does I'm in a bit of trouble."

"Not to worry." Millie pulled a cheese knife out of the drawer and started cutting. "Once we find the killer and prove this ghost business is a hoax, Myron will forget all about this."

"Don't be too sure about that, he's stubborn and he's been threatening Josie." Mom brought the cheese tray to the table and we all sat down.

"Speaking of which." I turned to Mike who had sat beside me. "What exactly did you tell him about the gazebo? He mentioned something about it when I saw him at the bank earlier and he did not seem happy."

Mike blushed. "Yeah, sorry about that. Anita Pendragon was nosing into the building permits and she saw my notes about the gazebo not being safe and making sure guests knew it was off limits. I guess he overheard us talking. I didn't realize he'd think it was a big deal, because it's not."

Millie waved her hand dismissively, the chunk of cheese atop her cracker wobbling precariously as she did so. "Of course it's not a big deal. Anyone can see the place is falling down so anyone with half a brain would steer clear."

"Yeah, except I saw footprints near there. The ground is a little muddy and the mud was tracked onto the boards. So, it appears someone was there recently," Mike said.

"Victor mentioned something about talking to Jed at the gazebo. Maybe he was scoping the place out," I said.

"Probably trying to make sure the setting was dramatic enough. Wouldn't put it past him to be the one that made the fake ghost noises. You know, to set the stage, so to speak," Millie said.

As if on cue, Nero and Marlowe appeared, circling us like vultures waiting for a morsel of cheese to drop. Mom snuck a pinch of Gouda to them.

Mike shoved a cracker in his mouth. "So *that's* why Anita was so interested in the gazebo. I'm sure she's planning on trying to get a scoop."

"She mentioned that she was in cahoots with Victor," I said.

Millie's left brow quirked up. "They're working together?"

I nodded. "To get in on this movie deal apparently."

"Ha!" Mom said. "I don't trust either one of them. I once heard Anita say she'd kill for a big scoop and I wouldn't put anything past Victor."

"I don't think Anita killed Madame Zenda though, because they were working together in the beginning. She was Anita's ticket to the big scoop." I reached down to pet Nero, who was tapping at my ankle. He dodged my hand and trotted toward the back door. Just like him to pretend like he wanted something, then walk away when you gave it to him.

Millie snorted. "So Anita *says*…"

"Let's consider this logically," Mike said. Mom and Millie looked surprised at his words. It almost sounded like he wanted to help us investigate. Odd, because the last two times there was a murder he seemed against our involvement. Maybe he was mellowing. "Who are your suspects and what are their motives?"

"Well, there's Anita because she wants a big story," Mom said.

Meow.

Meroo.

The cats were meowing at the door so Millie got up to let them out. "And Victor, of course. He wants a movie deal or something."

"And let's not forget Esther," I said, glancing out the window to see the cats sitting in the yard staring at me. "She seems nice, but she also seems very competitive with Victor about talking to Jed's ghost."

"So you think the motive is this movie?" Mike pressed his lips together. "Seems kind of far-fetched, doesn't it? I mean, it's not even a done deal. Murder is pretty extreme."

"You might be right," Mom said. "Didn't all these people know each other before? Esther knew Madame Zenda's name was really Betty Sue Lipowitz."

Mike nodded. "Ahhh so a previous connection. Maybe the death had more to do with that. Some kind of revenge?"

Meroooolow…

The cats muted meows filtered through the window and I saw them pacing back and forth near the overgrown grass at the edge of the lawn. "But she's not the only one who knew her. Look." I got my laptop from where I'd stashed it on the counter in the butler's pantry. The picture of the cruise was still up on the screen. "This cruise was a few years ago. You can see in the picture right up front, the featured psychics are Madame Zenda, Esther Hill and Victor Merino."

"Huh, how about that."

"Yeah, and Esther was at the bank. Did you know they have a display of older items there? It's bank history and such."

"You mean like buckles?" Millie asked.

"No buckles, but Belinda May gave me an envelope for Esther." My attention was drawn to the window again. Now the cats were twitching their tails and looking over their shoulder at me. I had the feeling I should go out there but not until we were done going over the clues.

Millie's brows shot up. "What was in it? Buckles?"

"No, just paper. I'm not sure exactly what was on it though because I was trying to get that out of Esther when the ghostly moans happened."

"Speaking of which." Mom stuck a slice of Swiss on a round cracker and then topped it off with another cracker. "Where did the ghostly noise come from?"

"Sounded like it was from outside. In the back," Mike said.

"How would someone do that? We were all in the foyer." Mom bit into the cracker sandwich.

"Remote control?" Millie turned to Mike. "Is that possible?"

"Yeah, sure. Lots of things are possible these days. There'd have to be a speaker of some sort though, to allow the noise to carry."

"That sounds like a lot of trouble to go to, and how would they work the remote without us seeing them?" Millie asked.

"Maybe they put it on a timer?" Mom suggested.

Millie squinted at the picture on my laptop. "So Esther and Victor knew Zenda…"

"And that tea-leaf lady, Gail." Mom pointed to a face in the back row of the picture and Millie squinted even harder. It was Gail.

"I didn't even notice her!" I said. "I was so focused on the names of the other psychics listed on the bill and she isn't one of them."

"Yeah, what is she doing lurking in the back there?" Mom asked.

Speaking of lurking, she'd been doing that in the butler's pantry too. She'd said she was looking for tea, but now I wondered. "She seems to lurk a lot. And Anita thought it was suspicious that she didn't have much of a history as a psychic."

"That *is* a bit odd. Maybe she's new? I mean, people have to start out somewhere. Look at Millie and me. We weren't ace detectives last year. We had to learn the ropes." Mom chewed a piece of cheese thoughtfully. "Then again, Gail was the only one who wasn't in the foyer when the ghostly noises happened."

Millie, Mike and I stared at her. She was right. I glanced out the window to see the cats trotting down the path that led to the gazebo.

"Maybe she wasn't there because she was at the gazebo orchestrating the noises." I pushed up from the table and headed toward the door. "And if she was, she might have left some evidence!"

Chapter Twenty-Two

"We better hurry, it's getting dark," Millie said as we followed the cats down the narrow path that led to the gazebo. It was still daylight, but the sun was starting to dip below the trees behind us as we picked our way through the overgrown grass, saplings and small shrubs.

It only took about five minutes to get to the gazebo. It stood on a highpoint of land and had a view of Smugglers Cove in the distance. The ocean was a hazy light blue, the sky pink with the reflection of the setting sun behind us.

The gazebo had seen better days. To say it was dilapidated was an understatement, though I'm sure it was once beautiful. I could see evidence of gingerbread molding in the corners, fancy lattice underneath and copper flashing on the roof, but all of that was now hidden beneath rotting boards and peeling paint. Grass and shrubs had grown up along the sides, vines wound around the railings and a thin tree had sprouted on one of the benches and grown through a hole in the roof.

It wouldn't be this unsightly for long though. Ed would start work soon and it would be grand again… if my loan held out.

A flock of pigeons flapped out of the crumbling cupola noisily as we approached. Millie stopped a few feet from the structure. "Look! Footprints!" She pointed to the mud where various partial impressions of shoes could be seen. I tried to make out what types of shoes. Surely that would help us figure out who had been here? The work boots were probably from Mike and Ed. There were others too, which looked like some sort of soft-soled tennis shoes. Millie took out her cell phone and snapped off a few pictures.

The cats had trotted off to the side and were sniffing around under the stump of a large oak tree. Nero glanced back, catching my eye. Was there something of interest over there? But no sooner did I wonder that than the cats came trotting back and sat down next to me, staring at the footprints as if they, too, were considering them as evidence.

Mike pressed his lips together as we all studied the prints. "There are more prints than when I was here before."

"Someone else has been here!" Mom said, as if she wasn't stating the obvious.

We'd seen Myron lurking near the barn from the upstairs window. I turned to survey the landscape, I could barely see the barn roof through the overgrowth, it wasn't close, but if Myron wanted to see the property up close he might have walked here from there or been here first. "Maybe Myron?"

Mike squatted down to look closer at the prints. "I don't think so. He wears dress shoes all the time and I don't see a print that matches that. Looks like work boots and some kind of tennis shoe or sneakers. Small size, so probably a woman."

Exactly what I had concluded. Too bad I hadn't said that out loud, I could have shown him that you don't need to have a past as a navy investigator to made logical deductions.

Merooooo. Nero and Marlowe hopped up onto what was left of the gazebo railing and sat, their tails twitching as they looked down at us.

Millie squinted up at them, then her gaze fell on the stairs. "Look there's mud on the stairs. You were right, Mike, someone has been in the gazebo."

Mike smiled indulgently at his aunt.

"But why?" Mom gave the structure a critical look. "The place is falling apart. Why would someone risk getting hurt by going in there? I mean, you could get splintered, or lockjaw or a broken leg."

"Must be something of interest in there." Millie gingerly picked her way up the broken steps. "And there's only one way to find out what that is."

Mereee!

Nero and Marlowe jumped down from the railing and headed to the other side of the gazebo, scurrying under one of the built-in benches that lined the walls.

"Better not go up there…" Mike's warning was too late, Millie was already at the top step.

"I think the cats are trying to tell us something." Millie rushed over to the other side where the cats were now waiting.

Mike sighed and started up the steps.

"Yep, footprints over here too!" Millie yelled. Her knees popped as she crouched down beside the cats. They were zigzagging back and forth, their interest centered on something beneath the bench.

"Better not mess around up there, Aunt Millie. It's not safe!" Mike probably knew she wouldn't listen to him. I mean, even I knew that when Millie was hot on the trail of something she didn't stop for anything.

"Oh, it will be fine." Millie's voice was muffled because she had her head under the bench. "Besides, the cats want to show me something."

Not wanting to be left out, Mom and I scurried up behind Mike. The first thing I noticed was muddy footprints and they weren't ours because the mud had dried. The second thing I noticed was that the cats were pacing back and forth atop the bench that Millie had her head under.

The third thing I noticed was that Mom had joined Millie and now both of them had their heads under the bench. There must have been a hole in the floor because Millie's right arm was digging around for something.

"I think I see something shiny under here," Millie said. "Do you see it, Rose?"

Mom stuck her head further under to the sounds of more joints creaking. She was practically lying down trying to get a good look into the opening. "There it is! To your left."

Mike and I exchanged exasperated looks.

Mike bent down and tugged at Millie's left arm. "Here let me do that. You shouldn't be doing this at your age."

Uh oh... that comment was going to backfire on him. Millie sprung up, hands fisted on her hips. Mom backed out of the hole and looked up at Mike incredulously.

"I thought I raised you better than that! Talking about a lady's age. And besides, I am not old!"

Mom jumped up and brushed the dirt off her pants. "Yeah, we aren't old! I'm surprised at you, Michael Sullivan." Mom reverting to using Mike's full name was not a good thing.

Mike didn't seem fazed. He crouched down and felt around under the bench. At least his remark had done the job of getting them off the floor. Perhaps Mike was more clever than I thought.

Mike pulled a small black-and-chrome device out from under the bench. "Huh, looks like a tape recorder."

"Aha!" Millie grabbed for it. "This must be what made the ghostly noises!"

"Someone hid it under that bench," Mom said.

Mike took it back from Millie and looked it over. To me it looked just like a small black box with some switches, like a cell phone.

"Let's see if you're right," Mike said. "This is a pretty simple device, looks like it just records and then plays back." He glanced toward the house. From here you could just see the top of the roof. "But I don't think the sound would carry all the way to the foyer of the guesthouse."

"Poppycock. It has to!" Millie grabbed for it again, but Mike pulled it back. "Let's hear what's on it."

Mike fiddled with the switches and studied the display. Finally, he pressed a button but all that came out was a repeat of the conversation we'd just had.

"You must have messed with it and put it on record. You have to rewind it." Millie grabbed it out of his hand and fiddled for a few minutes, but still the only thing it had on it was our conversation.

"Maybe we recorded over it, or the perpetrator set it to automatically erase the sounds after it played," Mom said. "You know, destroy the evidence like how the secret message would self-destruct in that movie *Get Smart*."

"Maybe." Mike didn't look convinced. "At any rate, someone did put it here for a reason. Unless it fell out of a pocket or something. Maybe we should call Seth Chamberlain."

"And what? Tell him we found a tape recorder with nothing on it?" Millie asked. "I'm sure he'll rush right over."

Meow! Nero was at the top of the steps, looking over his shoulder at us. Clearly he wanted us to head back to the guesthouse with the evidence. Marlowe was already halfway down the path.

"See? Nero has the right idea. We need to confront the perp with this. We'll pretend like the evidence is still on there and get a confession." Millie headed down the steps.

"I don't think—" Mike's sentence was interrupted by an alarm on his phone. He dug it out and looked at the display. "Shoot. I have an appointment for an inspection over on Glendale. I have to go."

"Darn. That's too bad." Mom hurried down the steps after Millie. "You're going to miss all the fun."

"Hey, wait up!" Mike jogged to catch up to Millie and I followed behind. I hoped he wasn't going to give us his lecture about not investigating. "Aunt Millie, don't forget the person who hid this might be dangerous. Don't do anything rash on your own," Mike said.

Millie stopped and turned faux-innocent eyes on her nephew. "Oh don't worry, we won't do anything rash without you."

He looked at her skeptically, and with good reason, as from where I was standing I could see she had her fingers crossed behind her back. I purposely avoided eye contact with him.

Mike sighed. "Hey, you're grown women."

"That's right," Mom said. "We can handle ourselves. Now you run along and we'll just take this tape recorder inside for safekeeping."

Chapter Twenty-Three

As soon as Mike walked away, Millie charged towards the kitchen door. "Any idea where we could find Gail this time of day?"

"Why are you so sure the recorder is from her?" Mom asked.

"I'm not, but she's the only one who wasn't in the foyer when the noises were made and she's mysterious. No background in the business and lurking behind Madame Zenda in that cruise photo. I say we question her first."

Mom hesitated at the door. "You did tell Mike—"

Millie cut her off. "I told him we wouldn't do anything rash. This isn't rash. This is calculated. And besides, there are three of us and only one of her."

We checked around the house and found Gail in the back parlor staring into a dainty blue teacup. She must have gotten that one out of the china cabinet, another one of the items that had come from Millie's family and been included with the sale of the guesthouse. I hoped Millie wouldn't be mad that the guests were helping themselves to the use of her family heirlooms.

Gail looked up, her eyes wary as we approached. Maybe she sensed our purpose, or perhaps the tea leaves had warned her.

Mom was making pointed glances at Gail's shoes and I looked down to see that the white fabric of her tennis shoes was stained dark from mud. Gail had been at the gazebo. I looked around the room for a weapon, just in case.

She smiled nervously and held the teacup in front of her as if for protection as we each took a seat. Mom sat on the sofa next to her and Millie and I each took one of the wingback chairs across from the sofa.

"Good afternoon, ladies." Gail glanced out the window. A gray twilight had descended and she amended her greeting. "Or should I say good evening."

"Evening." Millie was sitting so that the tape recorder was hidden. Probably saving it so as to have the element of surprise. It seemed quite obvious to me that she was taking pains to hide something and it must have been obvious to Gail too, if the way her eyes kept flicking to Millie's side were any indication. "I suppose you heard about the excitement."

"Esther told me about the ghostly moans." Gail huffed. "Probably that pompous clown Victor staged it as more drama to his big announcement."

Though I wouldn't put it past Victor to do that, I'd seen the look on his face in the foyer and he had appeared genuinely frightened. Of course, that could all just be part of his act.

"Yeah, funny thing though," Mom said. "We were wondering *how* he did that."

Gail shrugged. "Who knows? They have all kinds of gadgets these days that can produce such sounds."

"You should know about that, dear," Millie said.

At Gail's confused look, Millie whipped out the recorder and shoved it in front of her face.

Gail took a nervous sip of her tea. "That one doesn't seem suitable for the noise that I heard described."

"Ha! You would say that." Mom leaned closer to Gail. "That device is yours. Admit it!"

"Well… I don't know that it's mine… I do have one similar."

I was surprised at her curious reaction. I'd expected extreme denial or some kind of fight. Maybe she was thinking she could outwit us. I guess she didn't know Mom and Millie very well.

Millie leaned closer to Gail, she was practically out of her seat. Gail shrunk back into the couch, her eyes darting between Mom leaning close on one side and Millie leaning close on the other.

"Fess up. We know you were the only one not in the foyer when we heard the noises, and we found this recorder in the gazebo," Millie said.

"And you have mud stains on your shoes." Mom pointed at Gail's feet. "I bet that's the same mud that's out near the gazebo."

"And we know you were on that cruise with Madame Zenda. You have a previous connection!" Millie said.

"Yeah, one that might hide a motive for murder," Mom added, with a knowing nod.

"Hey, wait a minute," Gail said. "Esther and Victor were on that cruise too."

"But you are the only one who wasn't upfront about your purpose there. We saw a photo, and Esther and Victor were front and center as featured mediums and you were lurking in the background," Millie said.

Gail fidgeted. "I'm not hiding anything. I wasn't a medium on that cruise."

Millie tapped the recorder. "So you're saying you didn't hide this in the gazebo?"

Gail was silent, her eyes darting between the three of us as she gnawed her bottom lip. Finally, Gail slumped back on the sofa. "You're right. I am hiding something."

"I knew it!" Millie whipped out her cell phone. "I'll just call the sheriff now. Won't he be surprised to find that we've gotten the confession from Madame Zenda's killer!"

"Confession? No!" Gail put her cup down on the coffee table and I quickly shoved a coaster under it. Not for nothing, because the coffee table was antique mahogany and it was almost impossible to get those white rings out. I'd heard Flora complain about that plenty of times.

Gail continued, "I didn't kill Madame Zenda. That's not why I'm here. I'm here because of Victor."

"You were planning to kill Victor?" Mom must have taken a dim view of Victor, because she looked as if she was considering letting Gail go.

"No. I was here to prove he was a fraud. That's why I put the recorder in the gazebo." Gail gestured toward the device in Millie's hand. "I didn't put it in there to *play* ghostly noises, I put it in there to *record* Victor."

Millie raised a brow at her. "You did?"

"Take a look at it. You'll see it's on *record*. And it's blank, so you won't find any ghostly noises."

Millie, Mom and I looked at each other. We'd already messed up the original setting, but that would explain why all that was on it was the recording of our conversation.

"But what were you going to record?" Millie asked.

"I was going to prove once and for all that Victor was a fraud. He said he'd talk to Jed's ghost and mentioned the gazebo and the cemetery. I put recorders in both places hoping I could pick up something that proved he was a phoney. They are voice activated," Gail said.

"So you have a beef with Victor. I admit he is obnoxious. And those stupid velour suits. But what about the cruise?" Mom asked.

"And why is there no record of you being a psychic?" I gestured toward the teacup. "Most everyone has a website or some kind of ad, but you have nothing."

Gail looked down at the floor. "I'm not really a tea-leaf reader. I came out here on that pretense to trap Victor. Mary Chambers was my best friend. We were on that Dreams Divinity cruise together. That's where she met Victor."

It all clicked. I should have realized it before. Anita had said Gail was from Ohio and so was Mary. "Mary was the woman that Victor bilked out of money, claiming he could talk to her dead husband, wasn't she?"

Gail nodded, her eyes moist. "Yes. She was a lovely person and she *so* wanted to talk to her husband again. She died broken-hearted when her daughter convinced her that Victor was cheating her and she hadn't really been talking to her husband."

That explained why I'd seen her staring out the window at Victor and why Anita had seen her following them when they'd talked to the movie producer. If Gail's story was true, she'd been looking for dirt on Victor all along.

"Well then, who killed Madame Zenda and made the ghostly noises?" Mom asked. "Someone had to hide something somewhere to make them. Unless there really is a ghost."

Millie gave Mom an annoyed look at her suggestion that there might actually be a real ghost, then narrowed her gaze at Gail. "Maybe you killed Zenda by mistake, thinking she was Victor?"

"Hardly. There was no mistaking one for the other, and besides, I wasn't going to kill Victor, just prove he was a fraud so the whole world would know." Gail tapped her fingers on her lips. "But I did see one person doing something odd on the grounds when I was putting the tape recorder in the gazebo. I was sneaking around so no one would see me and so was the other person."

"We know all about Anita Pendragon lurking around," I said.

Gail shook her head. "No, it wasn't her. I hate to even mention it because she seems like such a nice person, but she really was acting odd." Gail looked up at us.

"Who?" I prompted.

"It was Esther Hill and she was messing around in that old outhouse. I have no idea what she was doing, but she was in there for quite some time."

Chapter Twenty-Four

"It's always the nice ones who have dark secrets," Millie said as we headed toward the outhouse, flashlights in hand. Now that the sun had set, the dark shadows of twilight loomed around us and the hooting of owls and scurrying of squirrels and chipmunks in the leaves took an ominous tone.

"I should have connected the dots earlier," I said. "Flora said Esther was at the outhouse, remember? I thought she was just doing her usual complaining about cleaning, so when the ghostly noises happened I didn't put two and two together, but the noise came from that direction and it would be a great place to hide something."

"Easy to see how you would think that. She does complain a lot." Millie flicked her light at the shabby structure as we approached.

The outhouse was fairly large and it wasn't in very good shape. It was listing to one side, the wood gray and rotting. Grass and weeds had grown up knee high around the outside. The door had a crescent moon cut out, but it was too dark in there to see inside. We creaked the door open slowly.

Nero and Marlowe pushed through ahead of me. The moonlight slanted in from the door opening and reflected off the cats' eyes as they sat blinking at us from the darkness inside.

"Well don't just stand there, let's go inside." Mom aimed her light at the interior and pushed in front of me.

"What do you think Esther was doing in here?" I asked as I pointed the beam of my light around. The flashlights were all small pen-sized lights that sent out a narrow beam that didn't reach far. Probably not that great for the job but, seeing as I hadn't anticipated skulking around in outhouses in the middle of the night, they were all I had on short notice.

"Hiding the speaker that made the ghost noises, of course." Millie shot me a look that said "duh".

"We shouldn't jump to conclusions. Maybe there is another reason she was here." I pointed my light at one of the holes. Nothing but a black pit. I dared not look too closely, that hole led to things I didn't want to think about. "Maybe she thought being here would bring her closer to Jed. I mean, he probably spent a lot of time in here and I do remember someone mentioning that being close to places or things that someone spent a lot of time near when living could help raise their ghost."

"This is an odd place to hide the recorder," Mom said. "Maybe Gail was lying to us. If I were the killer I'd lie to us."

"But Flora saw Esther here, too," I reminded them.

"And the recorder that Gail had didn't have ghostly noises on it," Millie said. "Her claims about the real reason she is here do make sense. We know Victor scammed that woman from the cruise. We should find a way to verify that she really was that woman's friend though."

"Even so, she could still be the killer." Mom seemed reluctant to let go of that theory as she ran her light over the three holes. "Sure glad we don't have to use this thing. Did you have to when you were a kid, Millie?"

Millie snorted. "I'm not that old! We had indoor plumbing. This old thing hasn't been used since my grandfather's time."

Meow!

Nero was walking along the "seat" part, which was just a long board with three large holes in it. "Don't fall in there, because I'm not going in after you." I used my sternest tone, but Nero just blinked at me and continued walking along, balancing precariously on the edges of the holes as if challenging me.

When Nero moved, my light picked out a spot in the wood that looked like it had fresh scratch marks. "Look at this, looks like someone pried this open."

"A hidden compartment, maybe?" Millie put her flashlight in her mouth and reached over toward the wood. She tugged and pulled and finally a small section slid back revealing a dark hole.

"What's in it?" Mom asked.

We all shone our lights into the dark section. "Can't see. The compartment goes behind the board." Millie angled the light and craned her neck to see inside. "Darn. It's too dark in there."

"Reach in with your hand," Mom suggested.

"I'm not reaching in with my hand, *you* do it." Millie stepped back from the hole and gestured for my mother to step up.

Mom looked at the hole uncertainly. "I'm not doing it. Josie, you do it. You're younger and if something bites you, you have a much higher chance of recovery." Mom pushed me toward the hole.

Visions of nests of spiders, centipedes or worse ran though my head as I aimed my flashlight inside. Someone had to reach in though, and I didn't want Mom or Millie to get hurt. Guess it was up to me.

I slowly put my hand in, tentatively feeling the sides and bottom of the compartment, my heart thudding with the expectation of feeling the creepy sensation of insect legs at any moment. Thankfully I didn't, but I also didn't feel anything of interest. Satisfied that I'd explored the entire compartment, I withdrew my hand as quickly as possible. "It's empty."

"Darn!" Mom said.

Millie shone the beam of her flashlight over the interior of the outhouse again. Probably looking for more secret compartments.

"Esther must have come in and gotten the recorder after the noises played. She'd have had plenty of time and we wouldn't have seen her because we were busy with Gail."

"But how would she know there was a secret compartment in the first place?" I asked. Still not convinced, I shone my light on the scratches again. The scratched wood was light, almost white in color. Surely it had been done recently.

"Good question," Mom said. "Maybe it wasn't Esther. Maybe it was Jed's ghost. He'd know about the hiding place I bet."

"Rose, there's no such thing as ghosts!" Millie who had had her back to us, turned quickly, the flashlight under her chin lighting her face in a ghastly way.

Mom screamed and jumped back.

I did too.

Nero and Marlowe practically fell into the holes they were circling.

Millie cackled, then lowered the flashlight and rolled her eyes. "Come on, let's look the rest of the place over. It's pretty obvious someone has been in that hidden compartment, but there might be another clue and we might as well look while we are in here."

We searched for a few minutes but found nothing else. The cats weren't much help, they were more interested in sniffing the holes. Yech.

"Well, I guess that's that. We need to confront Esther." Millie brushed the dirt off her hands and started for the crescent-moon door.

Merooo! Nero sounded like he wasn't too keen on confronting Esther. It was no wonder, she'd given the cats a lot of treats and they were probably reluctant to think she could be a killer.

"She did seem to get really mad when Victor claimed he was talking to Jed tonight," I said.

Merope! Marlowe added her two cents as I ushered them out of the outhouse and shut the door.

"And she got that mysterious envelope," Mom added. "We need to see what's in there."

"Yeah." Millie picked up the pace and was practically jogging toward the guesthouse. I wasn't sure if it was because it had gotten even darker and a little scary outside or if she was excited about facing Esther. "The contents of that envelope could be the key. I have a feeling that the sooner we find out what it is, the sooner we can catch our killer."

"I haven't seen Millie move this fast in years," Nero said as they trotted along beside the humans. Moonlight lit the path, but the humans had their flashlights bobbing in front of them like oversized fireflies. Blades of tall grass whipped Nero in the face every so often when he strayed too close to the edge.

"She seems eager to get on with her interrogation." Marlowe glanced back longingly at the outhouse. "It's a shame because there were lots of lovely smells in there and I hated to leave."

"They didn't even notice that someone had been digging at the gazebo," Nero said.

"We did all we could to alert them, but once they found the recorder they were focused on that."

Nero shook his head. "Just like humans not to consider there might be another thing to investigate."

"At least they got it half right. Gail did put the recorder there," Marlowe said.

"But who did the digging?" Nero asked.

"It could have been Gail. She was there."

"No, I think it was someone else. Perhaps Victor. He was missing from the guesthouse this afternoon."

Marlowe glanced at Nero. "Before or after the noises? Maybe he was the one hiding the recorder. It would make sense because he wants everyone to think he is talking to Jed."

"Indeed. I wonder if, perhaps, he was burying the recorder so as not to be found with the evidence."

"Or maybe he really did talk to Jed and was digging up the treasure," Marlowe suggested.

"There is no buried treasure!" Jed's voice boomed from beside Nero, making him jump sideways in the air like a frightened kitten. He then leaped and pivoted, trying to pretend he did that on purpose.

"Thought I saw a snake," Nero said at Marlowe's amused expression.

Marlowe turned to Jed. "You keep saying there is no treasure, but your memory doesn't appear to be very good. Maybe you are mistaken. I mean, you couldn't remember where you had buried it."

"That was just a momentary confusion on account of the property being so different from my time. Now that I have my bearings, I know exactly where I put things."

"And Esther tried to dig it up, but nothing was there," Nero added. They were almost at the house now and he wondered what Millie was going to do. At the rate she was moving she planned to go in all guns blazing and accuse Esther. That might not be the best course of action, especially since he had his doubts as to whether Esther was the killer.

"It wouldn't be there." Jed floated along keeping pace beside them. "I remember that old oak tree. There was no gazebo at the time, but the view of the cove is very pretty from that spot so everyone used to go there. I wouldn't be so stupid as to bury treasure there where anyone could stumble across it."

"So what was the digging at the gazebo about?" Marlowe asked.

Nero shrugged. "Another mystery to be solved."

"So you say that Millie and the gang think Esther is mixed up in the murder now?" Jed asked.

"She *was* in the outhouse for suspicious reasons," Nero said.

Jed stopped abruptly. He looked quite disturbed. "She may have had very good reasons. After all, I spent a lot of time in there."

"Umm… Okay. So she wanted to be close to you in an outhouse?" Marlowe's whiskers twitched. "Yech."

"The fact remains that someone took something out of that old compartment." Nero turned to Jed. "Did you know about that?"

Jed swirled and dipped. "I might have had a little secret stash to hide some hooch from the missus back then."

Nero exchanged a glance with Marlowe. "So you knew it was there, and you're in communication with Esther… so…"

"No! It's not like that. Esther is no killer, I swear to that!"

Poor Jed, he had it bad for Esther. Nero had never seen a ghost so smitten. Was Jed so gullible that Esther had him doing her dirty work? How far would he go for her?

"I don't think she's the killer, either," Marlowe said.

Nero glanced at the younger cat. "Is there concrete evidence which has caused you to reach this conclusion or do you just favor her because she gives us treats?"

Marlowe's steps faltered. "I… well… She seems so nice, I can't imagine her killing anyone."

"In our line of work, we can't go with how we feel, we have to make conclusions based on evidence." Nero tried to keep the exasperation out of his tone. One minute Marlowe seemed as if she was making great progress in the ways of becoming a cat detective and other times it was as if she'd taken two steps backwards. Oh well, not every feline could be a great detective like he was, he had to remember to be patient with his protégée.

Jed swirled to Esther's defense. "She is nice. And kind. She wants justice. Have you not considered that there may be another reason for her activities?"

They reached the house and Millie ripped the door open and ran inside with the other humans quickly following. Jed held back and Nero paused, waiting for him to fill them in.

"Well, what is her other reason?" Nero said finally.

Jed looked a bit unsure of himself. "I'm not sure exactly what Esther has in mind. Wait, it can't be..." He paused and looked off in the distance, then said very softly, almost as if to himself, " Yes... Yes... it all makes sense now. This goes back much deeper than either you or the humans think and I bet I know who is behind all of it."

Chapter Twenty-Five

Millie skidded to a halt in the kitchen and we all piled in behind her. The door banged shut, leaving the cats outside. They wasted no time in meowing their displeasure and I opened it to let them in. The five of us stood around catching our breath.

"What's your plan?" I asked Millie.

"I do think we need to proceed with caution. We could be dealing with a killer," Millie said.

"Maybe we *should* call Seth," Mom suggested.

Millie pressed her lips together. "No time for that, if Esther is the killer we need to act fast. Victor is planning something and I'm sure Esther means to stop him."

Meooow. Nero blinked up at us as if contributing to the conversation.

I looked down at him. "I know you like her, but this is bigger than cat treats."

Nero seemed affronted. He yowled, turned his back end toward us and flicked his tail at me.

Millie frowned at him. "Anyway. I'm sure she is still in the house, probably waiting to make a move on Victor. I think the key is to catch her alone."

"Good plan. Even if she tries something, it is three against one." I pointed to Mom, Millie and then myself.

"And two cats," Mom added.

"Right," Millie said. "I think we should get her to show us what was in that envelope and potentially use that to get a confession. I have Seth on speed dial so we can call him in once we have solid evidence."

"Good thinking. We wouldn't want to call him prematurely lest we ruin our reputation," Mom said.

Millie nodded. "We have to be very careful about our credibility. We've called him in on a few false leads before. Won't make that mistake again."

They were worried about their *credibility*? I was more worried about another murder at the guesthouse.

Millie put her fingers to her lips with a shushing noise. Someone was rustling around in the butler's pantry. We crept over to see Gail looking out the window.

Gail turned to us. "Shh… he's out there. I saw him."

"Who?" Mom asked, ducking down and then peeking up over the countertop to look out the window.

"Victor." From the tone of Gail's voice, she might as well have been telling us the devil was out there. I guess she did see him as such. I really hoped he was the killer, he seemed like a jerk, but the evidence we had pointed to Esther.

"What's he doing?" Millie asked.

"Getting ready for his fake talk with Jed, I assume. He called in that reporter," Gail whispered.

Anita Pendragon was out there too? I leaned closer to the glass but it was dark out and I couldn't see a thing.

"Tonight is Victor's last chance. I heard Anita saying the movie producer called her about the story. Nothing sensational has happened, so he's moving on. Victor will have to up his game." Gail turned to us, her eyes deadly serious and maybe a little crazy. "He may do something drastic. Maybe even murder."

"You think he's the killer?" Mom asked.

Gail turned back to the window and murmured, "I wouldn't put it past him."

Mom, Millie and I exchanged looks. *Should we try to follow him?*

"Here he comes!" Gail whispered as I saw a figure emerge from the shadows and head toward the back foyer.

We all ducked.

"What do you think he's up to?" Mom whispered.

"Not sure." Gail peeked up over the counter. "He must be setting things up for his big chance. Anita is out there too. I saw another shadowy figure over by the conservatory and it wasn't Victor."

The door to the foyer opened and we heard someone slip in. Sounded like they were trying to be quiet. Gail turned to us. "Are you going to catch him?"

Millie thought about that. "If he's the killer we will. But first things first, these things must be done in a methodical manner. Do you know where Esther is?"

Gail cocked her ear toward the ceiling. We could hear Victor going up the stairs. The second-floor landing creaked but he kept going. Was he going to the attic? I'd locked the door, hadn't I?

Gail didn't look away from the ceiling as she spoke. "Esther's in the front parlor gazing into that crystal ball of hers."

Millie jerked her head in the direction of the front parlor and said, "Come on, ladies. We have no time to waste!"

Esther was in the front parlor just as Gail had said. She was seated at the oak table next to the window, her gaze fixated on the crystal ball, which was practically glowing atop the purple velvet cloth she'd laid on the table's surface. I wondered if the cloth was part of her act or if she'd done that so as not to scratch the antique table. If it was the latter, I made a note to make sure to let her know I appreciated that… after we got a confession out of her, of course.

The cats were already there. They must have come in when we were talking to Gail. Marlowe was curled up on Esther's lap and Nero was sitting on the corner of the table, his gaze fixed out the window.

Esther looked up at us, her eyes cloudy as if she were somewhere else entirely. Slowly her gaze cleared and her face registered surprise.

"Oh, hello." Her voice sounded uncertain. I suppose it was a bit intimidating to look up and see the three of us looming over her.

Mew. Nero blinked at us. I sensed disapproval in his demeanor. Marlowe let out a snore from the comfort of Esther's lap. I envied Marlowe's ability to lapse into a catnap quickly and at any time, she was clearly oblivious to the gravity of the situation.

"Hi, Esther." Millie's tone was friendly as she sat down across from her.

"Would you like a reading?" Esther waved her hands over the crystal ball.

"No. We'd actually like to talk to you about something much more important."

"Oh?" Esther's gaze flicked between the three of us. "Yes. Those ghostly noises we heard earlier."

Millie sat back in her chair and studied Esther.

"Those were dreadful, weren't they?" Esther shivered.

"We think whoever is responsible must have hidden a device outside on the grounds," Millie said.

"Oh? I hadn't thought much about that." Esther was a good liar. She really did look as if she hadn't thought much about it. "I suppose they did. My guess is it was Victor."

Millie drummed her fingers on the table, the sound muted by the purple cloth. "Maybe, but you were also seen outside in a very odd place."

Meow! Marlowe stirred in Esther's lap and something crinkled. The envelope from the bank? I looked over but she had a flowy caftan on that hid whatever was crinkling.

Marlowe glared at Millie, then stretched and jumped up onto the table next to Nero and followed his gaze out the window.

"Me?" Esther averted her gaze, focusing on the crystal ball. "I have no idea what you mean."

Millie glanced up at me with a triumphant look. Esther was clearly lying and to Millie that meant she was the guilty party.

Mom leaned over the table. "Give it up, Esther. We know you're hiding something."

Mew! Nero's tone held a warning, but it wasn't directed at my mother. His gaze was steady out the window and… wait… someone was out there! I leaned forward to get a better look.

"I'm not hiding anything!" Esther was indignant.

"No? Then explain what you were doing in the outhouse!" Millie demanded.

"I had my reasons, which are none of your business," Esther said quietly.

Outside something was moving. A shadow. I leaned even closer. It was Anita Pendragon! I could make out the shape of her hair and it looked like she was wearing a trench coat. Rather dramatic if you ask me. What in the world was she up to?

Muffled creaking came from above. With a sinking sensation, I realized that I *had* left the door unlocked. Had Victor really gone into the attic and if so, what was he doing?

"I think you have way too many secrets." Millie leaned across the table. "Is one of those secrets the fact that you killed Madame Zenda?"

"What? No. I did not kill her." Esther's hands fell from the table to her lap.

"Well then, you won't mind explaining why you lied about being at the antiques store," Millie said.

"And what you purchased while you were there," Mom added.

"Or what is in that envelope that you got from the bank." I nodded toward her lap.

More crinkling. We had her now, she seemed rather nervous, her eyes darting to the crystal ball as if seeking advice from it.

"It's not anything to do with the murder. Well, at least not Madame Zenda's murder." She clutched the envelope to her chest.

"Let us see it, then." Mom grabbed a corner and tugged.

Esther tugged back. "It's just information from the bank."

"Good. Then you won't mind if we look at it." Mom tugged harder and Esther pulled back harder.

Something fell from Esther's lap to the floor and rolled under the table. The hardwood floors in the guesthouse were quite old and things had sagged a bit. Anything that fell on the floor eventually rolled to the middle. Nero and Marlowe were on it like alley cats on mice, their paws batting it to and fro.

I was hoping to see an old buckle, but no dice. It was a pen. I picked it up. It had a modern pen tip, but looked quite old, similar to the one I'd seen in the picture at the bank where Jed was signing something. Esther must have had Agnes Withington retrofit it.

"Aha!" Millie pointed at the pen.

"So you *were* at the antiques store," Mom said.

"So what if I was?" Esther tugged the envelope back into her possession.

"You lied about it and *that* means that you have something to hide," Millie said.

"I didn't have anything to hide. Agnes didn't want me to tell anyone."

"Why?" I asked.

"I gave her a reading." Esther gestured toward the crystal ball. "Some people are funny about that. We traded services, I did a reading and she made an old fountain pen I had from my mother into a more useable product."

I looked at the pen in my hand. "And you didn't buy an old buckle?"

"No." She sat straighter in her chair. "Now, if you are done interrogating me, I have much to do before Victor puts on his little show."

"I bet you do." Millie nodded knowingly. "Like making sure he doesn't have a chance to do it at all!"

"You have it all wrong!" Esther's voice quivered slightly.

Meow!

Nero and Marlowe scrambled up onto the table as another shadow passed. We were all looking out the window when creaking from overhead drew our attention to the ceiling. Mom seized the opportunity to reach over and grab the envelope, Esther tried to snatch it back, but she didn't quite make it and the contents spilled out over the antique Persian rug.

I snatched up the papers. Surely this was the clue to it all? But it wasn't, it was exactly as Esther had said—just old papers about the bank.

Esther shot up from her chair and shoved her hand in my face. "Give those back, they're nothing to you."

"Still feigning innocence. You might as well confess now. Josie will prove you're the killer with what is on those papers." Mom looked back at me with the utmost confidence. "Won't you, Josie?"

I barely glanced up at my mother. I was too busy trying to figure out just what it was about the papers that tugged at my memory.

The first paper was the early history of the bank. It was a photocopy of an old piece of paper where someone had scrawled in blotchy ink a timeline of the first several months. I looked up at the top to see a date. I guess that must have been a diary of some sort, written by the bank's founder, Thomas Remington, judging by the signature at the bottom. It detailed the money he'd used to start the bank and the small building he'd rented from which to do business.

"Well?" Millie looked at me expectantly.

"I'm not sure. This is a photocopy of an old journal from when the bank was founded." I glanced over at Esther. She seemed resigned now, sitting back in her seat, no longer trying to get the papers back. Apparently she was too dignified to run now that we were about to prove why she'd kill Madame Zenda. If only I could figure out what this paper had to do with her plan and tie it into the murder…

I handed the paper to Millie and looked at the next one. It was a list of old coins similar to the ones I'd seen at the bank display. It was also in Thomas Remington's hand and there was quite an extensive list. The bank sold antique coins, but I doubted they would part with any of the original coins Thomas had brought. Did the coins somehow figure into the murder?

"Ha! Look at that. I guess old Thomas Remington had perfect timing." Millie glanced up from the first paper as I handed her the second.

"Why is that?" Mom had come to stand behind Millie and was looking over her shoulder. Esther was still seated but now she was looking into her crystal ball as if mesmerized. The cats were sitting on the table watching us.

I was barely listening to Mom and Millie's conversation, my brain busy trying to make sense of all this as I scanned the third sheet, which appeared to be an accounting of old Remington family heirlooms and their value. It was almost like a receipt.

"Well, he opened the bank the same year Jedediah Biddeford was determined to be missing in Europe. He would have been out of a job if he hadn't done that." Millie reached for the next sheet and I handed it over.

The final sheet was the etching of the Oyster Cove guesthouse with Jed. He was wearing the shoes with the buckle. His wife stood next to him and children and staff to the side. Now why did that keep cropping up? I looked up at Esther, our eyes locking. Suddenly I knew what Esther had been up to. We'd made a huge mistake.

Millie snatched the last piece of paper out of my hand, pointed to it and addressed Esther. "Now there! This proves you're the killer!"

"Yeah!" Mom agreed, then frowned and looked at me. "Err… could you explain just how it does that?"

"It doesn't—"

Thunk!

A heavy onyx bookend toppled to the floor from the second shelf of the bookcase cutting off my words. Good thing it landed on the rug, might have made a dent in the floor otherwise.

"What?" Millie wore an expression of quizzical disappointment.

Meooo!

Merooolow!

Meruuuus!

The cats screeched as they bolted into the hallway. I could hear their footsteps racing up the stairs.

Realizing they were headed to the attic, I shot out of my seat. "I know who killed Madame Zenda and it wasn't Esther. We better hurry or there may be another murder!"

We'd reached the doorway when the lights went out, stopping us cold. That was odd, there was no storm, why would the power go out?

Of course! It was the killer. We'd left our flashlights in the kitchen. Did we have time to get them?

And that's when we heard the scream.

Chapter Twenty-Six

The scream left no doubt that there was no time to fumble around for the flashlights we'd left in the kitchen, so we headed straight for the stairs. By now my eyes had become accustomed somewhat to the dark and the moon shining through the windows helped, not to mention the meows of the cats who were just ahead of us. Lucky thing I didn't have to try to fit the key into the lock. Then again, if I'd locked the door like I was meant to, I supposed we wouldn't be running up here to stop a murder.

As we rushed up the stairs, noises from above quickened our steps. The moonlight had splashed in through the windows in the main house, but windows were sparse in the attic, so it was nearly pitch black. Muffled sounds came from the very far end where I'd seen Jedediah Biddeford's trunk.

"Ooof... Arghhh..."

Not ghostly noises this time, these were coming from a human.

Mew. Nero's meow was soft but insistent, as if he knew it was urgent for us to move toward the sounds but that we might not want to let the killer know we were there.

I focused on the direction of the noise, I was sure it was the back corner now, but getting there was another story. The attic was full of piled up cast-offs and it was too dark for me to see the path. Taking the wrong one might be off course and I'd be too late.

I started in one direction, but then felt a cold resistance and backtracked.

"Oghhhh..."

Oh no, that didn't sound good. We were making slow progress; a few times I'd taken a step down the wrong path but had felt an odd cold resistance blocking me and then turned around.

Meroo! Marlowe didn't need to tell me we were almost there, I could see the dark shadow of a person moving about as if wrestling something that was on the floor below them. Then a sickening thud. "Aghshhhh…"

"Hold it right there. We have you covered!" Millie shouted from behind me.

"Look out… gaghhh… gun!" A man's voice came from the floor. Was he warning us or was this some kind of trick?

Esther trotted up behind us catching her breath beside me. "Wait, that sounded like Victor. I thought he was the killer!"

"No, it must be Anita!" Mom said. "I knew she was up to no good."

They were both wrong. "I'm afraid not, it's—"

"Shut up or I'll shoot!" a voice shouted. "It's unfortunate you're all here. Now I'll need to think up a new plan."

"Guess it's not Anita. Is there really a gun?" Mom whispered. "Maybe they're bluffing."

"And what is Victor doing on the floor?" Esther asked.

"I think he's tied up," Mom said.

"I wish I could see." Millie craned her neck forward beside me. "We need to surround him then someone can get him from behind."

Millie's idea about surrounding the killer was a good one, but now that my eyes were getting used to the low level of light, I could see that wouldn't be possible. He was in the corner, backed up against a tall bureau that had boxes piled high. Beside that, other pieces of furniture were jammed in all the way to the walls. There would be no way to get behind there easily.

"Maybe someone should go down and get the flashlights," Mom whispered. "I can sneak back without him noticing in the dark."

"Quiet, all of you!" The killer waved something in the air. A gun, or was it a bluff? "Get up against those bureaus, spread out so I can see all of you. Wouldn't do to have one of you sneaking off now."

My mind was racing—we had to come up with a way to distract him so we could overpower him. Maybe if I got him talking, he'd get distracted and it would give me time to think. "You won't get way with this, M—"

Zzzzpt!

The lights came on, temporarily blinding me. I blinked, trying to keep my eyes on the gun. Maybe now I could rush the killer and…

"Myron Remington!" Millie gasped, looking from Myron to me. "Did you know it was him, Josie?"

Well, at least I was right about that. Myron *was* the killer. Too bad Victor was also right… Myron had a gun and it was pointed at us.

Myron looked dazed and a little spooked. "Who turned the lights on?" He glanced around the room as if expecting some sort of specter to appear. Too bad he didn't loosen his grip on the gun.

On the floor in front of Myron lay Victor. He was tied up and he must have passed out… at least I hoped he was only passed out and not dead. The sound of someone gasping behind us drew our attention.

Gail stood behind Millie, looking over her shoulder at Victor on the floor. "I heard the noises up here. Did you capture Victor?"

"No, silly." Mom turned her so she could see Myron with his gun. "Myron did. He's the killer."

Gail frowned. "Victor doesn't look dead."

"He's not," Myron snapped. "At least not yet. I guess you can all go together now. I won't say I regret that. You're all too nosey for your own good."

Merooo! Nero sounded indignant on our behalf.

Mewooo! Marlowe agreed.

The cats were pacing around in front of Myron. I wasn't sure if they had a plan, but I certainly hoped so.

"You might as well give up now, Myron. There are many of us and just one of you." I gestured to our little group now huddled against a large mahogany server pushed against the wall.

"Yeah but I have the gun." Myron's lips curved in a sinister smile. Apparently he'd recovered from his shock of the lights coming on. I would have preferred they stayed out, at least that way some of us would have a chance of getting away, but now he could clearly see all of us.

I barely heard what Myron was saying as I was busy wondering how we could get around behind him. Maybe Victor would wake up and trip him? I couldn't count on that and now with the lights on he'd see if one of us broke from the group and tried to slip between the furniture to the back. Where was Flora when you needed her? Last time we'd gotten ourselves into a predicament like this, she'd snuck up from behind and clobbered the killer.

"Okay then, a little change in plans might be good." Myron looked confident in his new plan. "Hmm… I think I'll use Gail's vendetta against Victor here." Myron kicked Victor who let out a miserable groan.

"What do you mean?" Gail asked.

"Don't think I don't know about that," Myron said. "It's too bad that everyone will think that you became so obsessed with him that you burned down the guesthouse."

Millie's hands flew to her face and she gasped. The cats meowed. I felt a little disturbed at the prospect myself. Not just that it was my home and how I made my living, I was getting quite attached to the place.

"Oh, don't worry," Myron continued. "It won't be a total loss… except for all of you perishing during the fire. I'll put a nice big hotel or some condos here. I did notice a good spot for a pool where that old barn is."

So he *had* been scoping out the grounds! Though I guessed that was only a secondary reason for him being out in the yard earlier. "But that's not what you were doing outside earlier today, is it?"

Myron nodded at me as if approving of my skills of deduction. "Nah. I guess I can tell you now since you won't be able to tell anyone. I was hiding the speakers that made the ghostly noises."

"Why?" Millie asked. "I thought you didn't want ghosts to be associated with the guesthouse?"

Myron narrowed his gaze on Millie. "Ha! That's where you got it wrong. I'm not afraid of ghosts."

Esther stepped out of our little circle toward Myron. "It won't work, Myron… I told the police the truth."

Myron stared at her as if trying to decide whether or not to believe her.

"That's right. I have the proof of what really happened, and I got it from your very own bank." She stood a few feet from him, hands on her hips. Apparently she didn't care that the gun was pointed directly at her. "I did it for Jed."

The cats seemed agitated at this pronouncement and paced around her feet as if trying to protect her.

"Liar!" The gun wavered in Myron's hand. "The bank tellers only said that Victor was there getting old coins. He was planning on putting on quite a show."

"Figures," Gail muttered.

Esther shook her head. "Nope. I was there too and now I know the truth."

"I doubt that," Myron scoffed, but he was starting to look nervous.

"What truth?" Millie whispered. "How is Myron mixed up in this?"

"The papers…" I whispered to Mom and Millie.

"Papers?" Millie asked.

"The ones Esther had from the bank. You gave me the clue, Millie. You said it was a good thing that Thomas Remington opened the bank when he did because he would have been out of a job with Jed's death."

"Yeah, but how could a butler afford—" Millie's eyes widened. "Oh… the treasure!"

"What are you whispering about back there?" Myron demanded.

"Esther's right," I said. "We know the truth about the bank. It's no use. Let us go and the police will go easier on you." I wasn't really sure if that was true. In fact, I hoped they wouldn't go easier on him, but I always heard them say that on TV and it sounded good.

Myron made a face. "I was afraid this would happen. You and your mother and Millie are so nosey. What papers are you talking about?"

"Turns out your pride was your downfall," Millie said. "You had to display all the history of the bank and old Thomas' journal papers. That's how I figured it out. The timing wasn't right for him to raise that much money!"

I frowned at Millie. Did she just say that *she'd* figured it out? I guess it wouldn't matter much who actually figured it out if we didn't find a way to get out of this.

"Is that all you've got?" Myron asked. "Those papers don't prove anything and, since no one else will think to look at them, I don't think anyone else will put two and two together."

"Not just the papers," I said. I didn't want Myron getting any more confident than he already was. The best course of action was to get him feeling uncertain and then he'd be distracted and we could use that to our advantage. "It was also that pen."

He turned the gun toward me. "Pen?"

"Yeah, the carved ivory pen you left here that day you viewed Ed's work on the ballroom. You had it retrofitted for modern use by Agnes Withington, didn't you?"

"It's an antique and I wanted it to be of use. So what?"

"Yes, it is an antique. In fact, I saw it in an old etching, but it wasn't Thomas Remington who was using it. It was Jedediah Biddeford. So it made me wonder... how did the pen come into your possession?"

"Thomas must have stolen it!" Mom said.

"Yep, and if he stole that, he probably stole Jed's fancy shoes with the buckles too. Isn't that right, Myron."

Myron's confidence was faltering. This was my chance! Millie could take it from here, so I whispered in her ear. "Cover me and keep him talking."

Millie maneuvered herself in front of me and I backed up, slowly receding into the dim shadows. Myron was too distracted to notice when I slipped behind the server, crouching low so he wouldn't see me making my way to circle around behind him.

"So what if Thomas stole some things from Jed? He deserved them, working as a butler all those years for a pittance. He didn't have any nice clothes and he needed to look presentable when he opened the bank."

"So you put the buckle and the note on Madame Zenda to scare people off." Mom paused, then added. "But why use the Oyster Cove Guesthouse letter opener?"

"To scare people off, of course." Myron wiggled the fingers of his free hand in the air. "Make people think the ghost did it because he didn't want anyone in his house."

"That's why you kept coming over," Millie said. "You weren't checking on the progress of the renovations, you were checking to see if anyone had figured out the real truth. And maybe you were a little afraid that someone really had been talking to Jed's ghost."

"Ha! I ain't afraid of no ghost. But I did have to make sure no one found out the truth," Myron said.

"So you tried to scare us off with those ghost noises," Mom said. "How did you do that?"

"Remote." Myron sounded pleased with himself.

A large box blocked my path and I moved it slowly so as to make no sound as I thought back to when we'd heard the noises. Myron had seemed frightened, ducking behind Mom and Millie… or so I'd thought. Now I realized he'd actually been hiding back there so no one would see him work the remote.

"But where did you put the recorder that made the noises? We looked everywhere," Millie said.

"Oh, I bet that's what he was doing out by the barn!" Mom answered.

"That's right, too bad you figured it out too late." Myron's voice took on a sinister tone and my heart pounded as I wedged myself in between a marble-topped bureau and a Victorian sofa with most of the horsehair stuffing exposed.

"But why?" Mom asked. "Everything happened three hundred years ago."

"Because if they knew the bank was started with stolen money they could take it away. The heirs, those cheesy guests you had here a few weeks ago, might try to get the money back. I couldn't risk anyone finding out the real truth…" Myron was starting to sound manic.

I quickly pushed another box out of the way and suppressed a sneeze. My quest was stirring up a lot of dust and I wasn't making much progress, I just hoped I'd get behind Myron in time to do something.

"The real truth?" Millie sounded confused.

"That's right, its worse than stolen money!" Esther's voice had a triumphant ring to it and I popped my head up over a cherry Chippendale server to see that she'd broken from the group and was standing a few feet from Myron, her hands fisted on her hips. She looked round at the corners of the ceiling and projected her voice as if speaking to someone other than those of us present in the room. "Myron's ancestor, Thomas Remington, killed Jed and put him in the wall. Then he dug up Jed's treasure and used it to start the bank."

"Oh, you don't say," Mom said.

"And that's why Myron had to stop Madame Zenda… and now Victor… from telling the truth. He's the killer!" Esther yelled.

"Fine, it's true! And since my ancestor is a killer, then a few more dead bodies won't matter!" Myron grabbed Esther and pulled her in front of him, pressing the gun to her temple.

Esther cried out.

The cats wailed.

I froze in place, not sure what to do. I was too far away to get behind Myron in time! Then I saw something strange. The bureau behind Myron started to shake, the boxes on top wobbled and then they started to topple, one by one as if an unseen hand was pushing them over.

Thunk!
Thunk!
Thunk!

The boxes hit Myron on the head, causing him to let go of Esther. He batted at them as they fell. Millie and Mom rushed toward him and my heart leapt. The boxes weren't enough to render him unconscious and he still had the gun. What if one of them got shot?

The boxes had fallen around Myron, their contents spilling out on the floor. He was dazed but not out. Then the bureau gave one last wobble. A heavy, peacock-shaped alabaster lamp flew off and hit Myron square on the back of the head.

He crumpled to the ground and Mom, Millie and Esther dived on top. The cats joined them, Nero sitting on Myron's backside and Marlowe on his ankles.

I rushed behind the bureau expecting to see Flora, just like the last time we caught a killer, but no one was there. It was empty except for a cold breeze and a few droplets of moisture on the edge of the bureau. I made a mental note to have Ed check the roof for leaks. Looking down, I saw the only footprints in the thick dust were mine. I would have suspected the cats, but not even a paw print could be seen, and I could have sworn they'd been in front of Esther when the boxes fell.

I glanced over the top of the bureau to see that Mom, Millie and Esther had taken the gun. Myron was out cold. Victor had woken up and was looking around, confused. Gail was standing over him and I do believe she was thinking about giving him a swift kick.

The bureau lurched to one side and I noticed the front leg was broken. Is that what had caused all the toppling? Either that was a lucky coincidence or, perhaps, other forces were at work. I didn't have much time to think about it because just then I heard footsteps running in our direction. Anita Pendragon burst out from between a gilt-decorated armoire and a tall pine hutch.

She surveyed the scene, catching her breath. Her eyes went from Victor tied up to Myron lying on the floor. She whipped out her camera and started snapping pictures.

"I don't know what the heck you people are up to here, but it looks like I finally got myself a scoop!"

Chapter Twenty-Seven

Four days later....

The scent of molasses and cinnamon filled the Oyster Cove Guesthouse kitchen. Millie's Aunt Gertie's famous molasses cookies were in the oven, but they weren't for guests this time. All the guests had left, so the baked goods were just for Mom, Millie, Mike and me as we sat around the old kitchen table discussing the strange turn of events over the past week.

Nero and Marlowe were at their stainless-steel bowls in the butler's pantry enjoying a treat of salmon and looking quite pleased with themselves. They deserved the treat as we all felt they'd tried to help capture Myron.

"Hard to believe that Myron went to such lengths to cover up the original murder of Jedediah Biddeford." Millie stood by the counter with an oven mitt on her right hand, ready to grab the cookies as soon as they were done.

"He had to, otherwise the bank could be in trouble because the initial funds were from ill-gotten gains," Mike said. "He confessed to everything."

"He sure went to a lot of trouble. Imagine killing someone and leaving that note and buckle!" Mom said.

"And using the Oyster Cove Guesthouse letter opener as the murder weapon to scare people off. He must have nabbed that on one of his visits," I added. "He thought it through."

"Yep," Mike said. "He'll be going away for a long time. I heard the Biddefords are suing the bank to get the original value of Jed's treasure plus interest."

"Oh dear," Millie said. "I hope that doesn't affect Josie's loan on the guesthouse repairs."

"I think the bank will be okay," Mike said. "The Biddefords will settle for enough to get their cheese-sculpting business on track and make improvements. Plenty of money will be left. Myron's cousin is taking over bank operations, I'm sure he'll honor the loan."

"Actually, I'm not worried about that. I got a little windfall from Esther." I tapped the large manila envelope that sat in the middle of the table. I'd received it earlier that morning and was quite shocked at the contents.

Mew! Nero and Marlowe trotted over at the sound of Esther's name. The cats had meowed at the window for twenty minutes when she left three days ago. She'd turned and waved goodbye to them, then studied the house for a few seconds before getting into the airport shuttle. She'd said something funny to me about "not worrying about the grand old house" right before she went out the door, but I hadn't paid it much attention until the envelope arrived.

"What's in it?" Mom asked.

I tipped the envelope and a pile of hundred-dollar bills slid out, along with a note.

Mom gasped.

Millie dropped the oven mitt.

Mike frowned.

"Where in the world did that come from?" Millie asked.

"Remember the secret hiding spot in the outhouse?" I asked.

Mom and Millie nodded.

"Well, turns out Esther *was* in there. Somehow she'd figured out that there was a secret hiding spot in there and she found a bunch of old coins. I guess she didn't feel right keeping them and she sold them for modern currency and sent it to me to help with the repairs on the guesthouse." I pulled a note out from under the bills. "In her note it says that she fell in love with the house and hopes the money will go a long way to helping restore it to its former glory."

Mike angled his head sideways to read the note. "Huh. So, I guess she only *seemed* suspicious because she was looking for clues to the identity of Jed's killer the whole time."

"Yep," I said.

"Interesting. I wonder why she was so keen on figuring out who Jed's killer was and not as interested in Madame Zenda's killer?" Mike asked.

I shrugged. "It turned out that one led to the other, so it all came out in the end."

"Fantastic!" Millie bent down to pick up the oven mitt. "I knew that she wasn't the killer all along."

Now I was the one frowning. I seemed to recall that she was almost certain Esther was the killer, if the interrogation she was subjecting her to prior to us rushing up to the attic was any indication.

Mom was frowning at her, too. "But Millie, you said—"

Millie interrupted her with a wave of the oven mitt. "That's all water under the bridge now. Seth did commend us for catching Myron. Of course, he claimed he was just about to wrap up the case with his own evidence, but there's nothing like catching the killer with a gun in his hand pointed at the potential next victim."

"Speaking of which, I think Victor got off a little too easy," Mom said. "I was rooting for him as the killer."

The oven timer went off and Millie took the cookies out, talking to us over her shoulder as she scraped the cookies off the baking sheet with a spatula. "Gail was too. I know she was disappointed Victor didn't get arrested, but he didn't *do* anything. Victor did seem very upset by the whole thing, I wouldn't be surprised if he walked the straight and narrow from now on."

"I don't know about that. He did try to fake the whole communicating with Jed thing and even buried a cache of coins in a burlap sack near the gazebo so he could dig it up later and pretend he'd discovered the treasure!" Mom said.

"Ironically, he'd purchased the coins at Myron's own bank," Mike said. "He blurted that all out to Sheriff Chamberlain without prompting. I don't think he'd make a very good criminal. And burying the coins wasn't illegal, so I guess he goes free."

"Well, hopefully that will be the last we see of him. I would like to see Gail get her revenge for him causing such sorrow to her friend, but I suppose everyone can't get what they want. Karma will get him in the end." Mom tapped the town newspaper that had been sitting on the table. "Anita came out ahead, though. She did get her scoop—though it wasn't really the one she expected."

The front page of the paper had the large image of Myron lying in the attic surrounded by the boxes and the various items that had fallen out of them. The cats were sitting on his backside and it almost looked like they were posing for the camera. Underneath a large caption read: *Local Banker Thwarted by Ghost.*

Anita had told us afterwards that she'd seen a shadowy figure—which we realized was Myron—lurking over by the side of the house just before the lights went out. She figured it wasn't a power outage and went to the main electrical box, which was still located in its original position outside on the corner of the house, to investigate. It took her a while, but she figured out the circuits had been flipped and she turned the lights back on.

"Funny, though, it seems it took Anita a while to get up to the attic after turning the lights back on." Millie took a large crystal plate down from the cabinet and started arranging the cookies on it. "And what *was* she doing lurking around here anyway?"

"She was meeting Victor. She said he had told her something big was going to happen and she might want to cover it." I repeated what Anita had told me. "She claims she didn't know he was planning on faking everyone out with those buried coins. She said she turned the lights on and then came inside as it all seemed suspicious. She heard the noises, but it took her a while to figure out we were in the attic."

"Probably took some time to snoop around." Millie placed the plate of cookies on the table and we all took one.

"I see she's still working the ghost angle." Mike pointed to the headline.

"Yeah." Millie broke off a piece of her cookie and nibbled on it. "But the producer is no longer interested, seems he has a more interesting story developing in some little town called Mystic Notch over in the White Mountains."

"Well, it's all for the best, because Anita doesn't really have a ghost story here." I was sure there was no ghost at the Oyster Cove Guesthouse.

"Yes, but how did those boxes fall on Myron?" Mom bit into her cookie.

"The bureau leg was broken. I guess it must have been ready to let go and the added weight of all of us up there on those old floors must have shifted things in such a way that the leg buckled and the boxes toppled at exactly the right time." The timing *was* suspicious, but that was my story and I was sticking to it.

"Maybe the cats had something to do with it," Millie suggested. "If they jumped on the bureau, that could have been enough to cause the leg to break."

Meow. Nero blinked up at us with his intelligent golden eyes. I was certain the cats were at Esther's feet when the boxes toppled, but I didn't say anything.

"Funny that Myron faked all that ghost business the whole time. He must have really wanted to scare people off." Mom took a second cookie then paused with it halfway to her mouth. "Odd though, I wonder how he got things to keep falling off mantles and tables, even when he wasn't here."

I'd wondered about that too. "The house is old and settling and I think those things might have just fallen because things are uneven. Remember how Esther's pen rolled toward the center of the room the night we caught Myron? It's natural in an old house that things are uneven, right, Mike?"

"Sure, to some degree." Mike didn't seem as convinced at my explanation, but what else could it be?

"Of course that must be it," Millie said. "And I'm glad this business is over. No more talk of murders or ghosts. I could use a little break from investigating."

Mom scowled. "Well, I don't know about taking a break from investigating, but I'm glad there's a reasonable explanation for everything. After all, there's no such thing as ghosts."

Meow!

Thud!

The rolling pin, which had been on the counter, hit the floor. We watched in silence as it rolled toward the kitchen door.

"Well now." Millie got up, gingerly retrieved the rolling pin and put it on the counter. "I guess that proves Josie's theory about the house settling. As you can see, it rolled right toward the door. The counters must be a bit off level too. Maybe you should look into that, Mike."

"Maybe I will. I'd love to have an excuse to spend more time here." Mike's pointed look made my cheeks heat and I ignored him, focusing on the tangy sweetness of the molasses cookie. "Or maybe you'd like to get away from Millie's cooking and have dinner some time."

I almost choked on the cookie. "Maybe." I glanced at my mother. If she thought I was going on a date with Mike, she'd never let me live it down. But she wasn't paying attention to our conversation, she was busy frowning at the rolling pin that was now innocently sitting on the counter.

Mom shoved the rest of her cookie in her mouth, tilted her head and looked at the ceiling. "Yes, I'm sure that's it. The house is sagging. Has to be, since we all know there's no such thing as ghosts."

Nero pulled his tail in, out of the way of the rolling pin, which was picking up speed as it rolled toward the door. He glanced up at Jed. "Did you really need to do that?"

Jed smiled. "Sorry, just wanted to pull their legs one last time."

"One *last* time?" A hopeful tone crept into Nero's voice. Though he liked Jed well enough, he'd been secretly hoping the ghost wouldn't stick around.

"Yeah, now that I'm free I've decided to hang around with Esther. I'm meeting her out at an event at some haunted house in Noquitt, Maine." Jed winked at Nero. "Ha! We'll show them what a real haunted house is like!"

"I have to admit that was quite a feat you pulled off in the attic." Marlowe positioned herself at Mike's feet and stared up at him adoringly. She knew he couldn't resist that look and it usually resulted in a nice treat being handed under the table. "And here we thought you could only move small objects."

"I thought that too! But when my Esther was threatened, I found the strength. I just couldn't let that nasty banker hurt her! And to think Esther did all that and risked her life just to figure out who my killer was." Jed beamed with pride.

"For a while I thought the killer might have been your wife's ghost," Nero said.

Jed ducked behind Millie's chair. "Where?"

"I didn't say I saw her, I just thought maybe all these she-nanigans were her doing. You did say she couldn't be trusted." Nero put his paw on Rose's knee and was rewarded with a tiny piece of muffin.

"Seriously?" Jed glanced around the room. "I mean, I'm not afraid of ghosts or anything, but I am afraid of my wife…"

"Nah, she's not here." Nero glanced around, his senses on high alert just to be certain. Nope. No ghostly vibes other than Jed's.

"Oh, phew." Jed came out from behind the chair. "Yes, she might have been in on it with Remington. And to think my trusted butler did me in and if it wasn't enough to kill me and stick me in a wall, he stole my pen and my good shoes!"

"And the treasure," Marlowe said. "At least now everyone knows that treasure is long gone and people will stop coming here looking for it."

"Good thing Victor didn't get to pull off his little stunt of digging up the coins he'd buried." Nero hopped up on the bookcase and looked out the window. "The whole state would be here looking for more."

"That was clever of you to send Esther for your little stash that was hidden in the outhouse. Good thing no one else discovered it all these years," Marlowe said. "You could have told us it was there though."

"Sorry I didn't tell you. I was saving that for someone special. I'd hidden the coins there the night I buried the bulk of the treasure in the yard. I wanted to be able to get at some of my treasure. Couldn't go digging the main stash up every time I wanted some extra coin. Course, I never got to even use any of it myself. I meant for Esther to keep that money, but she said it didn't rightly belong to her. She loved this old house and wanted to see it fixed up like it was back when I lived here." Jed looked at Josie. "We trust Josie to do that."

Nero felt a rush of pride in his human. Josie might not be so swift in the area of cat-human communication, but she could definitely be trusted and Nero knew she was growing very fond of the guesthouse and would do right by it.

"So now that your killer has been named, you're free to go to the other side." Marlowe looked at Jed curiously. "But you choose to stay here."

"Indeed. There's nothing for me over there. But Esther and I have worked out a nice system of communication through her crystal ball." Jed checked the clock on the stove. "Speaking of which, I have to sail off now. Gotta meet my lady. It's been nice working with you cats. Perhaps we will meet again someday."

And with that Jed slowly dissipated, leaving no evidence that he'd ever been there except for a slight mist on the floor.

The humans were cleaning up the dishes and Nero and Marlowe trotted to the front parlor. They were in dire need of a catnap. All this investigating was tiring.

"At least one of the guests here really could communicate with ghosts," Marlowe said as she curled up in the blue velvet chair.

"I always knew Esther wasn't the killer. She was too nice to us." Nero chose a spot on the corner of the sofa. Resisting the urge to run his claws through the brocade fabric, he turned a circle, settling in with his tail wrapped around his nose.

"Yeah, but did you know who the killer was beforehand?" Marlowe asked.

"I suspected Myron," Nero said. "But of course I didn't want to say anything out loud. I mean, can you imagine if I'd suggested the whole thing stemmed from the fact that the butler did it? How clichéd! If on the off-chance I was wrong, I'd have been the laughing stock of the cat community."

Marlowe slitted an eye open and looked at Nero, then sighed and snuggled deeper into the chair. "I'm glad both cases are solved.

I'm looking forward to long restful days spent catnapping and chasing mice."

"Me too," Nero mumbled, already drifting off to sleep. "Hopefully it will be a good long while before another murder happens at the Oyster Cove Guesthouse."

A Letter from Leighann

Hi! I hope you enjoyed *A Purrfect Alibi*. If you did enjoy it and want to keep up-to-date with all my latest releases, just sign up at the following link. Your email address will never be shared and you can unsubscribe at any time.

www.bookouture.com/leighann-dobbs

I've always thought it would be great fun to be able to talk to ghosts, so I love to sprinkle them into my books. In my cozy little world, ghosts are never evil and always helpful. Cats too, though I know in real life cats are rarely helpful and always mischievous!

All best,
Lee

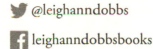 @leighanndobbs

leighanndobbsbooks

 www.leighanndobbs.com

Recipes

Homemade Turkey Sausage

This homemade sausage is not only delicious, but it's good for you too!

Ingredients:
- ❀ 1/2 pound ground turkey breast
- ❀ 1 egg white, beaten slightly
- ❀ 1/4 cup onion, chopped fine
- ❀ 1/4 cup apples, chopped fine
- ❀ 3 tablespoons quick-cook oats
- ❀ 1 tablespoon parsley, chopped
- ❀ 1/2 teaspoon salt
- ❀ 1/2 teaspoon pepper
- ❀ 1/2 teaspoon ground sage
- ❀ 1/4 teaspoon ground nutmeg
- ❀ Nonstick cooking spray

Directions:
1. Coat a 10-inch skillet with the nonstick spray.
2. Combine the egg white, onion, apples, oats, parsley, salt, pepper, sage and nutmeg in a bowl. Add the ground turkey and mix well.
3. Shape the mixture into patties and fry in the pan until meat is no longer pink and juices run clear. About 6 minutes on each side. Drain off the fat.

Lemon Muffins

Ingredients (makes 12):
- 2 cups all-purpose flour
- 1 cup granulated sugar
- 3 tablespoons baking powder
- 2 tablespoons grated lemon zest
- 1/2 teaspoon salt
- 3/4 cup milk
- 1/3 cup butter, melted
- 1 egg
- 1/4 cup powdered sugar

Directions:
1. Heat oven to 400 degrees F / 205 degrees C / Gas Mark 6.
2. Line a muffin tray with muffin cups.
3. Combine flour, sugar, baking powder, zest and salt in a medium bowl.
4. In a small bowl, combine butter, milk and egg. Mix well.
5. Add the wet mixture into the dry ingredients. Stir until just mixed. Do not over mix—you want the batter to be lumpy.
6. Fill the muffin cups 2/3 full and bake for 20 to 25 minutes.
7. Sprinkle powdered sugar over top and let cool.

Spinach Frittata

Ingredients:

- ❀ 1/2 pound spinach, chopped rough
- ❀ 1/2 tablespoon olive oil
- ❀ 8 eggs
- ❀ 1/2 cup whole milk
- ❀ 1 1/2 cups grated cheddar cheese
- ❀ 1/2 teaspoon salt
- ❀ 1/2 teaspoon pepper

Directions:

1. Preheat oven to 450 degrees F / 230 degrees C / Gas Mark 8.
2. Heat olive oil in oven-safe glass or cast-iron skillet and toss in spinach. Stir and cook for 2 or 3 minutes until wilted. Remove from heat.
3. In a small bowl, beat the eggs until frothy, add milk and stir.
4. Pour egg mixture into the skillet and sprinkle with the salt and pepper. Add the wilted spinach. Stir to combine.
5. Turn heat under skillet to medium and cook for about 5 minutes until the egg begins to set. Do not stir!
6. Sprinkle the cheese on top of the egg mixture and transfer the skillet to the oven. Bake 10 to 15 minutes until eggs are fully cooked.

Molasses Cookies

I admit, molasses is a little thick to work with, but there's nothing like the smell of molasses cookies baking in the oven.

Ingredients:
- ❀ 3/4 cup butter softened
- ❀ 1 cup brown sugar, packed
- ❀ 1 teaspoon vanilla extract
- ❀ 1 egg
- ❀ 1/4 cup dark molasses
- ❀ 2 cups all-purpose flour
- ❀ 2 teaspoons baking soda
- ❀ 1 teaspoon cinnamon
- ❀ 1 teaspoon ground ginger
- ❀ 1/2 teaspoon salt
- ❀ 1/2 cup granulated sugar (set aside)

Directions:
1. Preheat oven to 325 F / 165 C / Gas Mark 3.
2. In a large bowl, beat the butter, brown sugar, vanilla and egg, then stir in the molasses.
3. In a medium bowl, combine the flour, baking soda, cinnamon, ginger and salt.
4. Mix the dry ingredients in to the wet until well blended.
5. Roll 1-inch balls of dough in the granulated sugar then drop onto a greased or parchment-lined cookie sheet and bake for 12 minutes until the tops crack. Cool on a wire rack.